Last Laugh, Mr. Moto

BY JOHN P. MARQUAND

The Moto Series

YOUR TURN, MR. MOTO

THANK YOU, MR. MOTO

THINK FAST, MR. MOTO

MR. MOTO IS SO SORRY

LAST LAUGH, MR. MOTO

RIGHT YOU ARE, MR. MOTO

Selected Novels

THE LATE GEORGE APLEY

SINCERELY, WILLIS WAYDE

Last Laugh, Mr. Moto

JOHN P. MARQUAND

LITTLE, BROWN AND COMPANY

BOSTON   TORONTO

REPUBLISHED 1986

A serial version of this story appeared in *Collier's* under the title *Mercator Island*.

Library of Congress Cataloging in Publication Data

Marquand, John P. (John Phillips), 1893–1960.
    Last laugh, Mr. Moto.

    I. Title.
PS3525.A6695L27 1986   813'.52   85-31231
ISBN 0-316-54705-0

BP

*Published simultaneously in Canada
by Little, Brown & Company (Canada) Limited*

PRINTED IN THE UNITED STATES OF AMERICA

Last Laugh, Mr. Moto

CHAPTER I

WHEN ROBERT BOLLES tried to put all the events in order, his mind would keep going back to Mercator Island, although he knew that Mercator Island was nearer the end than the beginning. Sometimes when he awoke at night he would think of the warm air, and the spray, and the black water, and the way the mainsail of the *Thistlewood* drew. Somehow the important things, the terrible things — such as fear and sudden death — never seemed as important as all sorts of extraneous details — such as a joke that someone had made, or the way Tom had of never wiping the galley table clean. He would recall the strange slatting sound of the coconut palms near the beach. He would see the phosphorescence in the water around the roots of the mangrove bushes. He would even find himself thinking that Mr. Malcolm Kingman, which was the only name he ever knew him by, was a good companion according to his lights.

"Call me Mac," Mr. Kingman had told him, "and I'll call you Bob. It's easier, what?"

3

Then Bob Bolles would stare into the dark, and he would think of the pale blue of Mac Kingman's eyes. They had the steady, watchful look of a sailor's eyes, though of course he was not a sailor. And when he thought of Mrs. Kingman, for that was the name she was using, he would find himself still surprised at her capacity for enjoyment. It had impressed him long before he came to know her well. She had really loved it — all the lights at the sunrise, all the strange shimmering green of the hillsides, and the candlewood trees, and even the delicate little shells on the beach. She had loved it at Westerly Hall, when she had stood on the gray coral stone terrace, where all the weeds were growing and where the umbrella ants were walking in an endless, weaving column. She had said that she would like to live there always, and she had really meant it.

Even when he had heard the footsteps that night — and he had not heard them until they were just behind him — he remembered most clearly what a pleasant night it had been and how well he had played his hand of four spades, doubled and redoubled. Of course they had meant to kill him as soon as he had left the table, but it was those small aspects which remained more vivid than the rest.

"Bob," Mac had said, "your sense of cards is excellent."

"Such a nice hand," Mr. Moto said, "and to make the three of diamonds good! So very nice."

She was the only one who had not said anything.

"Hélène," Mr. Kingman had said, "you must be tired. Perhaps a little walk in the air — "

That was the first time that he had not called her "Helen" — just one of those slips which you could not help. It was all made up of little things like that, hundreds of little things.

There was no rancor, because it was all strictly business, and they had done it very nicely, because they were professionals. He could not get it out of his head that they really liked him as a person and as a human being, but it had not begun at Mercator Island. That was only the middle and the end.

It had begun in Kingston Harbor, when the *Thistlewood* lay anchored in the still blue water, on a November morning in 1940. He always hated the mornings. In the morning everything that was disagreeable came back to him, for he could never get himself into the way of drinking before twelve o'clock. All he could do was to sit and wait until noon came and assure himself that after twelve he would feel better and that by evening he would forget nearly everything that troubled him.

"Mr. Bolles, sar," Tom had called from the cockpit, "it's after eleven o'clock, sar."

"What the hell do I care?" Bob Bolles called back.

"You expressly ordered," Tom said, "when we came aboard last night, for you to be awakened at ten o'clock, sar."

"Don't talk with that damned British accent," Bob said.

Tom came down into the cabin and stood grinning at him. He was a lanky, Jamaican colored boy, copper-colored, with a small head, flat nose and heavy hands. He did not look like much, but he was good at sea.

"Where was I when you took me aboard last night?"

"Up to Henry's, sar," Tom told him.

"Henry's?" Bob said. He passed his hand over his chin and found there were no contusions or bruises on his face. "I wasn't fighting again, was I?"

"No, sar," Tom said. "You haven't fought, sar, since they threw you out of the Myrtle Bank bar. You were at the tables like a gentleman, and Mr. Henry came down to tell me you were cleaned out and that you had best be took on board. You came with me like a gentleman."

"Cleaned out?" Bob said. "Have you looked through my pockets?"

"Yes, sar," Tom told him. "Ten shillings and six is left, sar."

"All right," Bob said. "Haven't I told you to watch me at Henry's?"

6

"I endeavored, sar," Tom said. "You are most difficult when you are in liquor, sar, actually. You began talking about the Board, sar, and what you thought of that Old Man. You are always most difficult when you think of the Board."

"Well," Bob said, "all right." He had grown used to being on the strangest terms with Tom. Sometimes he thought that Tom knew more about him than anyone had ever known. "We're going to be short of money."

"They're loading bananas, sar," Tom said. "I could get work today and tomorrow."

"No," Bob told him and he felt half ashamed of himself. "I'm going ashore and you go too and find yourself another berth."

"Oh, no, sar," Tom said. "I like it here."

"And why the hell do you like it?" Bob asked him.

"It's the way you treat me, sar. White men don't often treat colored people like you treat me."

"Get me some coffee," Bob said, "and hot water and a razor. Bring them up topside so I can be in the air."

When he climbed up in the cockpit the white sunlight from the water made him blink. In the morning he sometimes felt ashamed of himself and he did not like the feeling. He had a pretty clear idea of what they thought of him along the waterfront in the morning. He stood in the center of the cockpit, in his last clean shirt and in his soiled white trousers. He had not shaved for two days and now he decided that

7

he might as well wait another day before he tried it.

"Stow the razor," he said. "Just the coffee."

He noticed that his hand was shaking when Tom handed him the tin cup of coffee, but he felt better when he drank it. All the waterfront and the harbor came together more clearly in focus.

"Coat," he said, "shoes — hat — and bring the dinghy alongside."

They were loading a banana boat at the pier. He could hear the shouts, and he could see the line of black men and women with the bunches of bananas on their heads. Then he looked toward the entrance of the harbor. A United States destroyer was coming in, gray and cloudlike.

"Tom," he said, "go down and fetch the glasses."

"You pawned them yesterday, sar," Tom said.

"Yesterday?" Bob repeated. "It must have been quite a day — yesterday. What's the number on her?"

"S-156, sar," Tom said.

"Just as I saw it," Bob answered. "That will be the *Smedley*. I wonder who's commanding. Get out the dinghy."

He stepped in and Tom took the oars.

"Where will you go, sar?" Tom said.

"Over to Henry's," Bob answered.

"Yes, sar," Tom said. "Henry's it is, sar."

It had always seemed to Bob Bolles that the waterfront of any port in the world was about the same as that of any other. Take St. John's in Newfoundland, for instance, or Cherbourg, or Haifa, or Singapore. The language and the complexion of the citizens might vary, but when you were near the docks you might as well be in Lima or Yokohama or Shanghai. There were the same tanks, the same smells and shipping, the same sounds of the donkey engines. The grog shops were the same and the pawnshops and the houses of doubtful reputation. Kingston was just like that to his eyes — no better and no worse. If he had been blind, he could have found his way by sound.

He lounged along the main street slowly in order to kill time, only because of his prejudice against drinking before noon. Above him the sky was pitilessly blue and clear, except for a few clouds which made deep green shadows over the mountains inland. The street was trig and neat, like all the principal streets in a British colony. The houses and shops were painted in pleasant stucco tints, like most buildings in the tropics, and the shops were behind arcades to protect the passer-by from the sun. A dusky traffic policeman in a faded khaki uniform stood at an intersection, but the traffic was slow and scattered. The tourist trade had dwindled with war times, but the shops waited hopefully. All the life in Kingston was moving dreamily and peacefully toward high noon. Tom, he knew, was following him because Tom always looked after him when he went ashore.

He paused to examine the British tweeds and pipes and Burberries in the window of one of the large clothing emporiums, and as he stood there he saw his own reflection in the window. The reflection suddenly seemed like the figure of a stranger — a heavy, shambling seedy figure in a soiled white suit. His face beneath his battered Panama hat was drawn and unattractive. Even the vague reflection showed the sandy stubble of his beard. It did not bother him that people looked at him curiously and disapprovingly. He knew that he was almost on the beach — not quite, but almost.

Beyond the clothing store was a newsstand and then a tobacconist, and then the bank and a square with tired-looking hack horses and sleepy drivers and women selling shells and baskets — but no one tried to sell him anything. Then there came a store displaying oriental goods, a store which you might see in any Caribbean port. In the window there were silk pajamas and bathrobes with dragons embroidered on the pockets, a few kimonos, some bad pieces of teakwood, tea sets and cheap soapstone and ivory ornaments — all the things they made by the boatload in China or Japan. A small Japanese wearing heavy glasses stood in the doorway and nodded to Bob Bolles.

There was nothing in the world quite like the manners of Japan. They were the manners which never varied in any life or setting. That brisk nod of the head was something which no European could imitate. It was vibrant with nervousness and with a set desire to please which completely concealed the personality behind it. Manners over there were a façade which covered everything. Bob Bolles had sometimes heard it said that all Japanese were alike, but he had traveled enough to know that this was a ridiculous statement. You could put Japanese in certain categories as easily as you could put Europeans. There was something about the little man standing there which was not of the shopkeeping type, something that was a little too neat and too nervous, the cheekbones and the mold of his chin too delicate, his hands, as he clasped them and bowed, were too fluttering and too graceful. For an idle moment Bob wondered how he had come there. There was so little you could tell about the Japanese. He might have been a student. Like all his people, he would have had military or naval service. He might have been a connoisseur of the arts. They could change from one thing to another. And there he was, standing in front of a shop.

"Hello, there, Admiral Togo," Bob said.

The little man drew in his breath with a gentle hiss.

"Or maybe you aren't Admiral Togo," Bob said. "Maybe you're Japan's Lawrence of Manchuria."

The Japanese smiled, displaying an uneven set of teeth shining with gold work.

"Good morning," he said. "Lawrence of Manchuria. Americans are always so very funny."

"So are Japanese," Bob said. "How's business, Admiral?"

"Business is very poor," the little man said. "Please, would you like to buy a new silk suit? To your measure by four this afternoon. So nice on that schooner of yours for yachting, please."

"Clever, aren't you?" Bob said. "So you know me, do you?"

"Please," said the little man, "of course. Mr. Robert Bolles, please. So nice to have watched you in Mr. Henry's last night."

"I never saw you hang around there," Bob said.

The shopkeeper laughed politely. Japanese always laughed politely. And he took a card case from his inside pocket.

"Please," he said, "my card. Pajamas and shirts and suits on six hours' order. No hurry to pay, please, Mr. Bolles."

Bob Bolles took the card with elaborate courtesy and held it gingerly in both hands and bowed. The card read *"I. A. Moto — Things Japanese."*

"Thanks," he said. "What time is it?"

"Please," Mr. Moto said, "it is a quarter before twelve."

"Well, that's swell," Bob answered. "I'm sorry. I'm in a hurry now. Good-by, Mr. Moto," and he walked more hastily down the street.

Henry's was down near the water, a pumpkin yellow café, with a bar and tables in the front room and with propeller-like fans moving languidly on the ceiling and with a shabby courtyard and other rooms out in back. The front room was deserted except for Henry who stood behind the bar. Henry was slender and very neat in a freshly laundered white suit. His features were aquiline and regular, made up from a variety of race strains. Bob sat down at a table and took off his hat and gazed upward at the slowly revolving fans.

"Bring me a bottle over here," Bob said. He was just in time — the clock on the cathedral was striking the hour of twelve — and he looked up at Henry and grinned. "I understand I was in here last night."

Henry nodded. Bob poured half a tumbler of rum and drank it straight.

"And now I'm not welcome here," he asked, "is that it?"

"Oh, no," said Henry, "I wouldn't say that, Mr. Bolles, but there has been a complaint."

13

"What complaint?" Bob asked.

Henry clasped his hands behind him.

"The police," he said. Bob Bolles scowled.

"What about the police?" he asked.

"Supervision is getting strict now," Henry said. "They've been inquiring about you, Mr. Bolles."

Bob Bolles looked at his empty glass and felt his face flush. It was the first time that anything like that had happened to him, but he could understand it.

"You mean, you're going to throw me out of here?" he asked.

Henry unclasped his hands from behind his back and spoke quickly, almost eloquently.

"You must think of the difficulties I have here, Mr. Bolles," he said. "The type of guests whom I entertain in back each evening require quiet surroundings. When gentlemen like you come, Mr. Bolles, who have allowed themselves to get out of control, the authorities — "

Henry stopped and Bob saw that he was looking toward the doorway. He remembered a long while later that there was something worried and wary in Henry's look. A youngish man had entered from the street and his passage from the sunlight into the shadow of Henry's bar made him blink with eyes which obviously were not accustomed to the glare of the Caribbean. His gray flannel suit and his light gray felt hat showed that he was a tourist and not an islander, a tourist too recently arrived to equip himself with tropical clothes. There was nothing impressive about his appearance, for he was the sort of person who would not have been conspicuous anywhere, but it seemed to Bob Bolles that Henry was surprised. There was something that Henry did not like.

"Good morning," the stranger said, and his greeting included Bob Bolles at the table and Henry standing beside him. "Is this a place that is called Henry's?"

"Yes," Henry said, "this is Henry's. I am the proprietor, sir."

The stranger smiled an engaging, easy smile. His hair and eyes were dark, but his complexion was light, almost pale, and it seemed to Bob that he looked a little tired and a little hungry. He glanced around the barroom, not casually the way a tourist might, but carefully, as though he wished to remember the location of all the chairs and tables.

"So you are Henry, are you?" he said, and his voice was foreign, rather more French than Spanish. "My firm has recommended you. I believe you have had some past connections with my firm."

"What firm, please?" Henry asked.

The dark young man took a wallet from his pocket and pulled a card from it.

"Wines and liquors," he said. "Lisbon, you see. My name is Durant."

Bob Bolles saw Henry take the card and, though

15

the interruption annoyed him more than it interested him, he saw Henry's manner change. Henry was always smooth and easy when he greeted guests, but he had a maître d'hôtel's way of conferring little distinctions, an elegance that did not always fit well in the barroom. Bob could see that the card had impressed Henry and that Mr. Durant was someone above the ordinary.

"Oh, yes," Henry said, and his hair looked particularly sleek and oily as he bowed and held out his hand. "So happy to meet you, Mr. Durant. Your firm's wines have been a great addition to my little place here, Mr. Durant. You were right in coming to see me. Should you like a room?" And then before Mr. Durant could answer Henry continued in his careful Jamaican English: "You understand that this is not a hotel, but for our especial friends we do have rooms upstairs, very nice and quiet. Also if you have any friends here I could put you in touch with them."

"Why, thank you," Mr. Durant said. "What I need is quiet. I'm looking for a man, a particular friend of mine. I imagine you have seen him, since he has been connected with the firm in the past — a Mr. Kingman."

Mr. Durant spoke pleasantly, with that slightly foreign accent, and Henry bowed again.

"Oh, yes," Henry said, "yes, he has been here. You

16

must be my guest, Mr. Durant, entirely my guest. Mr. Kingman is coming in later this morning, I think."

"Very good," Mr. Durant answered. "You are very kind. I understood you would be. When Mr. Kingman arrives I'd like to have a conversation with him. I haven't seen him lately, but he used to be quite a friend of mine."

"Why," said Henry, "there's nothing easier, Mr. Durant. I'll send him directly up to your room, if that is what you want."

"That is most obliging of you," said Mr. Durant. "Perhaps if you will show me the room I might go up now. My bag is at the airline office, if you will send for it. I am rather tired. I have just got off the plane."

"You did entirely right in coming here first," Henry said. "It's a nice room. Just one other guest upstairs — a Swedish gentleman, but I am sure he won't disturb you."

"A Swede?" said Mr. Durant. "What's a Swede doing here?"

Henry shrugged his shoulders.

"A mate from one of the banana boats," he said. "Just here for a rest. He won't disturb you."

"Well, let us go," said Mr. Durant, and he nodded at Bob Bolles and smiled, and Mr. Durant and Henry walked up a flight of stairs behind the bar while Bob

Bolles sat staring into his half-empty glass. He was glad that Henry was gone. It seemed to him that Henry's manner was particularly greasily unctuous that morning. It was none of his business, but there was always something mysterious about Henry's friends. He had seen other curious people come in and out of Henry's, but that was what you could expect in a gambling joint. He sat there waiting for Henry to come back, and he did not like it.

"Bolles," he said to himself, "you're mighty near on the beach."

CHAPTER II

WHEN Henry came back ten minutes later his hair was as slick as ever and his walk was sprightly, but Bob could see that Henry was worried about something.

"I didn't know you ran a hotel here," Bob said.

"What?" said Henry. "What did you say?" Henry was looking out the open door to the street and he seemed to have forgotten that Bob was there.

"I didn't know you ran a hotel," Bob said.

"Oh, not a hotel, really," Henry answered. "Just a place where a few personal friends sometimes stop." Henry drew a colored handkerchief from his breast pocket and patted his forehead softly with it.

"Oh," Bob said, "so this Durant is a friend of yours."

"A business acquaintance," Henry said. "Let me see. What was it we were talking about?"

"About the police," Bob said.

"The police?" Henry's hand moved with a quick, involuntary jerk and his colored handkerchief hung limply between his fingers.

"Yes," Bob said. "You were saying the police say I make too much trouble. Well, it looks as though a cop is coming in here now. That's Inspector Jameson, isn't it? How are they going, Inspector?"

Henry gave a startled look at the door. He had not seen the new visitor as soon as Bob had, but when he did Henry smiled and put his handkerchief back in his pocket. In Henry's business he naturally had an understanding with the island police.

"Oh," he said, "good morning, Inspector Jameson." A red-faced, middle-aged man in carefully tailored white ducks and with a close-cropped mustache and very square shoulders walked toward them. Inspector Jameson was carrying a swagger stick and he had the appearance of an English sergeant major. His uncompromising steadiness showed that he had been in the Army once.

"Hello, Chief," Bob said. "How's the Empire holding up this morning?"

"Now, now," said Inspector Jameson. "That will be enough of that. The Empire can do very well without being asked for by the likes of you."

"All right," Bob said. "It was just a courteous question. I like the Empire and I can't help being worried about it."

"Good morning, sir," Henry said. "A lovely day, isn't it?"

Inspector Jameson disregarded the question. He walked over to the table and halted, looking at Bob Bolles in a steely way.

"I don't like jokes," Inspector Jameson said. "If I had ever had you on parade, sir, you would have learned what was fitting. The trouble with the Empire is all the silly people — French, Germans and Americans."

"Yes," Bob answered. "How about a drink, Inspector?"

Inspector Jameson looked at the bottle on the table with stony distaste.

"No," he said. "This is an official call. I've been looking for you, Mr. Bolles."

"All right," Bob said. "Nice to see you, Inspector."

Inspector Jameson cleared his throat. His face was lined with disapproval and distaste. His voice was strictly official, according to regulations.

"Mr. Bolles," the Inspector said, "I am here on the line of duty and you know me and I know you. You have been here two weeks with your schooner, making, if I may say so, a problem of yourself when the police have other things to think about. And I don't want none of your lip either, Mr. Bolles. It was the same the last time you were here and the time before that. We have tried to make allowances, since regulations are to make matters happy for visitors on this island."

"But I am happy," Bob said. "I'm always happy. You ought to learn to relax, Inspector."

"None of that, sir," the Inspector said. "You are a man, sir, who should be a gentleman. Your kind is very bad, sir, when it goes bad. We have tried to make every allowance, but it will have to stop."

"Oh," Bob said, "will it?"

"It will," the Inspector said. "I should suggest that you and your boat and your nigger leave here in twenty-four hours."

Bob stood up. He felt his face growing red.

"Do you realize," he asked, "that you're talking to a United States citizen?"

The Inspector watched him, but he did not appear impressed.

"We know all about you," he said. "We know about every bit of riffraff that drops into this town. You'd be wise to remember what I said, Mr. Bolles. We should like it if you were not here tomorrow."

Inspector Jameson turned slowly on his heel and walked majestically to the street, while law and order walked invisible behind him. Bob Bolles had seen his kind before in a dozen other British colonies. He had laughed, but Inspector Jameson stood for the British Empire. He was the sergeant who looked after the black sheep in Kipling's poem. He was the thin, red line of heroes. He was Waterloo and Dunkirk. Bob Bolles looked up at Henry.

"The British can turn out a model," he said.

Henry did not answer. He was watching Inspector Jameson cross the street.

"You read about them," Bob said, "but you can't believe it. He doesn't think, does he? He just reacts. An Army man, isn't he?"

Henry did not answer.

"I never had a run-in with that kind before," Bob said, "except once when the ship called at Singapore." Suddenly his eyes grew narrow and he looked hard at Henry. "It couldn't be, not possibly — or could it — that you have been complaining to get me out of here?"

Henry shook his head.

"Oh, no, Mr. Bolles," he said. "Why, you and I are friends."

"Then lend me some money," Bob said.

Henry glanced toward the street. He had a habit of looking in all directions at once.

"I can do better for you," he said, "because I'm really a friend of yours, Mr. Bolles, and I can prove it. There was a party here yesterday, a nice young couple from New York. They want a yacht for charter. I spoke about you. I can get you four hundred dollars for a month."

"No one sails her but me," Bob said. "I don't want her piled up somewhere."

"You did not let me finish," Henry answered, speak-

23

ing quickly. "Four hundred dollars for charter, fifty dollars a week for yourself as skipper, twenty dollars for your boy as crew."

Bob Bolles whistled softly and poured himself another drink.

"Who are they?" he asked. "They're not your style."

"They were seeing the sights last night," Henry said. "They came down from the Myrtle Bank. Their name is Kingman."

"Kingman?" Bob Bolles repeated. "Is he the one your friend upstairs wants to see?"

Henry patted the folds of his yellow necktie and stood up a little straighter.

"I said they were a nice young couple from New York," Henry said. "Mr. Durant is a stranger to me and I am sure I don't know how he knows Mr. Kingman, and besides it should not matter to you, should it?"

"It just strikes me as funny," Bob said. "You say they are nice people."

"Well, they are," Henry said, "very nice people — New York socialites and very rich."

Bob Bolles laughed.

"No nice people hang out in this joint, Henry — just boys like me. You might find a murderer here, but not a New York socialite."

Henry's shoulders gave a little spasmodic jerk as

24

though someone had hit him on the back, but he was hurt rather than angry.

"You very well know," he said, "that a great many socialites come down from the hotel for roulette. There is a certain romance and color here that they do not find at the hotel. That was how I met Mr. and Mrs. Kingman — just down for the roulette. They are very romantic. They wish to take a private cruise, because they are interested in lonely islands. And they pay well. Money is no object. What more do you want?"

Bob wondered even then why Henry had been so generous as to offer him such a job, because it was not like Henry, but when a chance like that came out of the blue, all you could do was take it.

"All right. I'll take them if they're fools enough. What's your commission?"

"Twenty pounds," Henry said, "should be my commission, but for you it will be nothing. Shall I telephone them now to come here? You are hardly dressed to call at their hotel."

"Wait a minute," Bob said. "Why aren't you taking a commission? What is there fishy about this?"

Henry's face was always tranquil and it showed neither surprise nor hurt.

"Don't be a fool," he said. "Look at me. Can I afford to do anything fishy? I'll telephone them and perhaps you'd better go in back and shave." He picked up the bottle and the glass. "And you might at least say thank you."

"Thanks, Henry," Bob said. "But I'd like to know what you're getting out of it. Oh, well, never mind."

Henry rang a bell for a boy to watch the barroom.

"I shall telephone from my office," he said. "You can shave in my own washroom with my own razor. You see, I really treat you as a friend."

They crossed the back courtyard which had been planted with palms and bougainvillaea to form at night a garish electrically lighted garden and came into Henry's gambling parlor. The long room with its slot machines and chemin de fer and roulette tables seemed to be lying in a drunken sort of sleep waiting for evening. Louis, the croupier, and his assistants would not come on until evening and the room's only occupants were two barefoot colored women emptying ash receptacles and aimlessly brushing the floor. Henry's office, which was just beyond the tables, was furnished with a violent green carpet, two leather upholstered armchairs, a comfortable couch, and a battered roll-top desk and a telephone.

Henry sat down at his desk and lifted up the telephone receiver. "The lavatory is over there. You will find the razor in the cabinet," he said.

Henry's office and lavatory were both what Bob

expected, neither of them very attractive and neither very clean. A towel on the rack by the washstand was smeared with lipstick. The medicine cabinet above it was filled with headache remedies, perfume bottles, an atomizer, and hair tonic. He was not particular, but somehow the idea of using Henry's razor did not appeal to him. He could hear Henry calling the hotel and asking for Mr. Kingman.

"Hey," Bob called, "have you got any clean blades?"

"Is not the old one all right?" Henry asked. . . . "Yes, Mr. Kingman, please."

There had been a time when Henry had treated him with an obsequious sort of respect. Bob knew that it was his fault that the relationship was changed, and it irked him that the proprietor of a cheap saloon and gambling joint should be doing him a favor.

"Oh, Mr. Kingman," he heard Henry say, "I have the man here now."

Henry was speaking of him in the tone he might have used when he told a customer that he would have two jolly girls and an automobile ready in half an hour.

"Yes," he heard Henry say, "I believe he would be glad to leave at five o'clock. Yes, I'll have him waiting for you."

Bob wiped his face on the corner of the towel and walked into the office.

"Now you look quite the gentleman," Henry said. "They are coming right over — Mr. Kingman and his lady. It's lucky for you this happened."

"Yes," Bob said, "it's lucky."

Bob saw Henry's brown eyes examining his clean face and clothes.

"You're not wearing a necktie. I can lend you one."

"Listen, Henry," Bob said. "If they don't like me the way I am, to hell with it. What are you so damned anxious about?"

There was no longer much doubt that Henry was going to get something handsome out of it somehow. They were back in the front room again when a car from the hotel drew up by the door and a man and a girl got out. Henry hurried to meet them and the three walked together to a corner table where Bob was standing. Their clothes looked like models from an expensive store window in New York — just the thing for that winter cruise in the tropics. They had an air of plenty of money and of tourists' wide-eyed innocence, even before they spoke.

"This is the man," Henry said. "This is Mr. Kingman — Mr. Bolles."

Bob shook hands with Mr. Kingman, and Mr. Kingman's hand was cool and very strong. He was a good-natured looking man in his middle thirties with an easy, pleasant smile.

"Oh," he said. "I'm glad to meet you, Mr. Bolles."

28

His accent had a careless drawl and the words were clipped in a way that reminded Bob of a British-educated European's speech. It was the assured, hard-to-identify accent of a well-bred, widely-traveled man and Bob Bolles decided that he liked him. Mr. Kingman's nose was thin and a little too long, his complexion was pale but healthy, his eyes and his mouth were both steady. When Mr. Kingman looked Bob over, the smile on his thin lips was reflected in his eyes, and Bob could not have helped smiling back.

"We're — we're shot with luck to meet you, Mr. Bolles," Mr. Kingman said, and Bob Bolles always remembered how Mr. Kingman hesitated, seeming to grope for the right colloquial phrase. "Let's sit down and talk this over — with a bottle of champagne. This is Mrs. Kingman."

She was a tall girl, just the type he particularly liked. He imagined that she could dance beautifully. Her hair was dark, almost black, and her eyes were dark blue, and her face was tanned and healthy.

"How do you do?" Bob said.

She looked surprised when he spoke to her, as if she must have thought that he would be a good deal worse than he was.

"Oh, Mac," she said, "not champagne."

"Now, Helen," Mr. Kingman said, "this is our vacation, dear."

She looked at Bob, as though she wanted to be sure that he understood.

"He's been working so hard," she said. "Those New York law firms!"

"Leo," Henry called to the bar boy, "a bottle of Veuve Clicquot — on the house."

"Mr. Bolles," Mrs. Kingman said, "I feel so much better, now that I've seen you. You look so perfectly reliable — and this is one of Mr. Kingman's most absurd ideas."

Mr. Kingman smiled.

"Now, wait a minute, sweet," he said. "You know you promised, didn't you, to let me do the talking? Maybe I'd better give you a picture of what's in my mind, Mr. Bolles, before we get down to facts." He raised his glass and laughed. "It's simply that I'd like to get away from everything for a while — telephone, telegraphs, everything. Maybe you've felt that way yourself."

"Yes," Bob said, "I feel that way a good deal of the time."

"When you're a — " Mr. Kingman began, and his forehead puckered slightly as though he found a momentary difficulty in thinking of the next word — "a kid, you have ideas which sometimes stay with you. Do you know what I mean?" He looked around the table almost appealingly. "When I was a kid I always thought of the tropics — lonely islands, the Spanish Main — you know. Maybe you read about pirates yourself once, Mr. Bolles."

"You're in the right place for pirates," Bob said, and he glanced at Henry. Mr. Kingman seemed lost in his own thoughts.

"Those ideas stay with you sometimes — the sea, the loneliness of the sea. Now, back at home, I've done a lot of reading."

"And he never lets me interrupt him," Mrs. Kingman said, "never."

"Well, now I've got my chance," Mr. Kingman said. "I suppose it sounds silly to you, Mr. Bolles, but it came over me when I landed here, why not? Why not charter a comfortable boat and get off away from jazz music, off to islands that I'd read and dreamed about, where none of these cruises stop — off — " He paused again, as if trying to think of a word. "Off to loneliness."

He stopped and looked around the table, as though he had made a considerable effort and waited for an approving answer. Again Bob tried to analyze his speech. It seemed strange that Mr. Kingman kept striving to use colloquial expressions.

"There are a lot of lonely islands, if that's what you want," Bob said.

Mr. Kingman smiled happily at Mrs. Kingman.

"You know," he said, "this is just my luck, isn't it? Now, I don't know who you are, Mr. Bolles, from — from Adam, but you're just what I've been looking for. I think we're going to have a — a swell time. Don't you like him, Helen?"

"Yes," Mrs. Kingman said, "I do, Mac."

"There you are," Mr. Kingman said. "I hope you don't mind my being so informal, Captain, but it's just as well to like someone if you're going to sea with him. Now, they say you have a boat — "

"She's a schooner," Bob said, "sixty feet. I bought her in Key West about two years ago — the *Thistlewood*. She can go anywhere under sail, but she only has a small auxiliary."

"I don't want power," Mr. Kingman said. "I don't need to get anywhere at any time. You know navigation, of course."

Bob Bolles nodded.

"And you have a crew?"

"A colored boy," Bob answered. "We can take her anywhere you want. Have you any ideas, Mr. Kingman?"

Mr. Kingman leaned across the table.

"You know how things get in your mind," he said. "Now, I have been reading about the old sugar islands, where planters lived, each alone in his kingdom. It's all gone of course, but there must be remains of it. Perhaps you can help me, Mr. Bolles.

Have you ever heard of a spot on the chart called Mercator Island?"

Bob Bolles had no intention of looking surprised. If they had the money and were good for it he could have taken them to the South Seas, if they wanted. Nevertheless, the question interested him. Mr. Kingman must have known it was unusual, for he had introduced it by that elaborate explanation. You never could tell, Bob thought, where a romantic streak may crop up in a human being.

"Mercator?" Bob said. "I wonder where you ever came across it. I know a bit about Caribbean literature, but I never knew that Mercator got into print."

Mr. Kingman seemed pleased that he had asked him, anxious to explain.

"You'd have a hard time finding the volume, Skipper, even in the largest library," he answered. "I stumbled on it at a book auction, a rather rare collector's item."

"He fills the apartment with books," Mrs. Kingman said, but Mr. Kingman did not appear to hear her.

"*The Caribbean Kingdom,* by John Silverstone," Mr. Kingman said, "and more particularly the estates on the Winderly Group. Octavo, original calf, published by John Cotswell, stationer, at his shop in Threadneedle Road, London, 1773."

"That's right," Bob said, "the Winderly Group. Yes,

I've heard they used to grow sugar on Mercator."

"A queer old book," Mr. Kingman went on, as though he had not heard. "There were five pages about the sugar establishment and the life on Mercator Island. That's all I know, but I'd love to see it. Do you know it, Mr. Bolles?"

"I've never touched there," Bob said, "but I've been by the Winderly Group. It's about as lonely a piece of reef as you can hope to see. It's off every conceivable sea lane. I don't even know what flag it's under. It isn't very well charted. Mercator is about four miles long, volcanic with coral reefs outside it. I've heard the old planters were driven out in a slave insurrection. Have you ever heard about it, Henry?"

"Not much," Henry answered. "The fishing boats might know."

Henry's voice was soft. For some reason it made them all silent for a moment.

"But I don't want to know any more," Mr. Kingman said. "It is exactly that sense of mystery that I want. Ulysses cleaving the wine-dark sea. Let's be — be pushing off."

"Mac, dear," Mrs. Kingman said, "don't be so impatient."

"If you want to go," Bob said, "it's maybe four days' sail with a fair wind — longer, if it's stormy."

Mr. Kingman had forgotten about the wine-dark sea and suddenly looked practical.

"All right," he said. "That's settled, if the terms are satisfactory, and I believe you've heard them. What accommodations have you? Not that we aren't willing to rough it. There will be Mrs. Kingman and me and — and my valet. His name is Oscar."

"When I married Mac," Mrs. Kingman said, "I really had to marry Oscar too."

Bob Bolles looked at them doubtfully.

"I don't know how you'll fit in," he said. "There are two bunks in the main cabin and one berth in the owner's stateroom. Tom and I can sleep up forward, but we'll all have to eat together."

"Splendid," Mr. Kingman said. "Oscar and I can take the cabin. You take the stateroom, Helen. Let's — let's shake a leg. I'd like to leave this afternoon."

"It's a pretty tall order," Bob said. "I'll have to take on supplies."

Henry cleared his throat.

"I think I can get supplies aboard for you," Henry said, "if you will be willing to leave it to me."

"Good," Mr. Kingman said. "Now we're getting action."

"You haven't asked for references," Bob Bolles said.

Mr. Kingman laughed.

"Let's not mind that," he answered. "I've heard all about you and I've seen you. I think you're all right and I hope you think we are. All I want is to get off and get going." He pulled a pigskin wallet from the breast pocket of his coat. An American passport came out with it and he replaced the passport hastily. "Here's forty pounds — on the line."

"Thank you," Bob said. "That's thoughtful of you. I hope you will be comfortable, Mr. Kingman. I can meet you at four o'clock and take you aboard."

"I shall bring them to the boat," said Henry. "Just be ready there."

"That's fine," Mr. Kingman said. "Everything is going to be hunky — hunky-dory." He looked at Mrs. Kingman and laughed. "Sweet, didn't I tell you we could do it? Didn't I tell you we'd have fun? Oh — oh, boy, are we going to have fun!"

Bob Bolles turned to look at her. He was surprised to find that she was looking at him and not at Mr. Kingman. Her eyes were dark and watchfully questioning — but just for a moment, and then she smiled.

"Yes, dear," she said. "I suppose I'd better get dungarees and sneakers and oilskins. We won't have much time to get packed and I don't know the shops."

Mr. Kingman made an impatient gesture.

"Yes, I suppose you will — " he began. "There isn't anything more, is there, Henry?"

"Perhaps Mr. Bolles could take Mrs. Kingman for a little shopping turn," Henry said. "I only suggest it because — "

Henry's voice was smooth and unctuous, but Mr.

Kingman seemed to catch some message in it, for he looked at Henry and raised his eyebrows.

"Because what?" he asked.

"Just a little matter," Henry said, "about supplies, arrangements and payments. There is no need for Mrs. Kingman to wait if she is in a hurry. If I might suggest, Mr. Bolles can help her with her purchases and leave her at the hotel."

Mr. Kingman still seemed to hesitate.

"Is it necessary?" he asked.

"Just half an hour," Henry said. "I think it would be better." And he took a card from his pocket and handed it to Mr. Kingman. Bob Bolles remembered it. It was Mr. Durant's card. It seemed to Bob when Mr. Kingman looked at it that he was making an effort to keep his face good-natured, to conceal some sort of surprise or annoyance, but Bob Bolles was not sure.

"Oh, yes," said Mr. Kingman, "I see. Yes, we'd better go over the details, and it might be as well to find Oscar, but I don't like to have Helen wandering around alone — a strange town and all that."

"There's no need to worry," Henry said, "not with Mr. Bolles."

"All right," Mr. Kingman said. "That will be — be okay." He was smiling, but it seemed to Bob that his eyes had grown a trifle harder and his lips a trifle thinner. "If Mr. Bolles doesn't mind, Helen, you might go out. Buy out the shops — buy anything."

It seemed to Bob that Mrs. Kingman was looking at his shabby clothes and her dark eyes seemed to have the same questioning look.

"Someone from the hotel — " Bob began.

"Oh, no," said Mrs. Kingman, but she seemed to have lost her enthusiasm. "It will be all right. Come ahead, Mr. Bolles."

She stood up and they all stood up.

"See you later, Bolles," Mr. Kingman said, and he looked down again at the card he was still holding.

CHAPTER III

WHEN Bob stepped out on the street behind Mrs. Kingman he saw Tom sitting on the curbstone, waiting for him.

"Tom," Bob said, "get aboard and clean up. Put my stuff up forward. Here's twenty pounds. Get fresh sheets and towels. Be ready to take on supplies at three o'clock."

Tom looked blankly at the notes.

"It's all right," Bob said. "We've got a charter — " and he turned to Mrs. Kingman. "This is my boy Tom. He'll be on the boat with us."

"Oh," Mrs. Kingman said. Her whole manner seemed stiff and constrained. "Well, we'd better go on to the shops."

They began walking to the center of the town. It had been a long while since Bob had walked beside a girl as pretty as Mrs. Kingman and a girl of his own class. He found it hard to think of anything to say to her. He found himself making a few tentative remarks about the streets and buildings and about the best stores, but she only answered curtly.

"I suppose you'll get your commission in each place," she said finally. "That's customary, isn't it?"

Bob felt his face flush scarlet.

"I hadn't thought of it," he said. "I've never taken out a party in my boat before."

"I just wanted to find out," she said. "In there in that saloon, in that place, I couldn't make you out. So you don't take out parties regularly? What do you do?"

"Nothing," Bob said.

"Nothing?" she repeated. "You're an American, aren't you?"

"Yes," Bob answered.

"Well," she said, "I don't understand you. What are you doing here in a boat doing nothing?"

"Trying to get away from myself," Bob said. "Haven't you ever wanted to do that?"

She looked at him. Her eyes were dark. She looked aloof and beautiful.

"I don't know whether I like you or not," she said.

"You'll know before we get back," Bob answered.

"I don't know whether I trust you or not," she said.

Bob Bolles laughed.

"Do you always talk this way to everyone you pick up?" he asked, and she looked back at him without smiling.

"No, I don't, as a matter of fact," she said. "It's because you puzzle me. You look like someone who ought to be different from what you are, but I'm not sure."

"I haven't asked any questions about you," Bob said. "There won't be any occasion for you to have to trust me. Here's where you can get some oilskins and dungarees."

Just as they turned into the shop he saw her watching him again.

"I didn't mean to be disagreeable," she said.

"Oh, that's all right," Bob answered, and he stood near the door of the large, cool shop, watching her make her purchases.

"I wonder what's on her mind," he said, beneath his breath. "Why the devil does she have to trust me?"

He had never been in the position of a paid employee on a boat who could be patronized and treated casually, but he could not get it out of his head that there was something unusually odd about her and about Mr. Kingman and Henry. They had been too artificial, too neat, too nervous, and even when Mrs. Kingman had been talking to him it seemed to him that she had been thinking about something else. She was worried about something. In spite of the easy artificiality of their talk, all of them had been worried.

"Oh, Mr. Bolles," she called.

She was in the back of the shop, trying on an oilskin coat with a sou'wester on her head. "Is this all right?"

"Yes," Bob said, "that's fine."

"I look queer in it, don't I?"

"No," Bob said. "You're the sort of person — " and he stopped, because it was none of his business what sort of person she was.

"You're the sort of person who looks well in anything," Bob said, and then he found himself blushing.

"Well, that's everything here," Mrs. Kingman said. "I wonder if there's any place where I could get some silk — some Japanese lounging pajamas, if it's hot."

Then Bob Bolles thought of Mr. Moto. The card was in his pocket and the Japanese store was only a few doors down the street.

"Why, yes, I know the very place," he said.

He offered to carry her bundles for her, but instead she ordered them sent up to the hotel at once, and paid for them, as Americans so often did, in crisp new dollar bills at a ruinous exchange rate; but prices did not seem to bother her.

"I'll be glad to get away from here," she said when they were on the street again. "Will you?"

"Yes," Bob said, "I'm always glad to be moving. What did you mean when you said a while ago that you couldn't trust me?"

"Oh, that," she said. "You mustn't mind me. I say all sorts of things."

No one had ever told him what to do when you took your employer's wife shopping. He did not know whether he should walk behind her or beside her, but he did know from the way people looked at them that they made a peculiar pair. He was too down at the heel and too seedy to be walking with her. Something made him want to apologize for his appearance, but he did not see how it would help.

They passed Inspector Jameson just before they reached the Japanese shop. Bob saw the Inspector's eyes protrude slightly, and he laughed.

"It's all right," he said. "It's all right, Inspector."

"Inspector?" Mrs. Kingman said. "Is he a policeman?"

"That's right," Bob said. "I guess you don't know much about the authorities or you'd have spotted him. Why, Inspector Jameson ordered me off the island just this morning. I was in luck to meet you and Mr. Kingman."

He wondered if she would be shocked, but instead it seemed to him that Mrs. Kingman looked relieved and in some way amused.

"Why should he do that?" she asked.

"Why?" Bob said. "Generally disorderly conduct."

"Oh," said Mrs. Kingman, and she laughed. "Well, that's all right then."

"How do you mean, it's all right?" Bob asked.

"Oh, nothing," Mrs. Kingman said. "It just means

you're what you look like, and I'd rather have you that than something else."

"What do you mean by something else?" Bob asked.

"Oh, nothing," Mrs. Kingman said. "Is this the shop?"

They had stopped in front of the window with the Japanese embroidery and the curios. A little bell rang when they opened the door. It was a narrow box of a place with trinkets in a small glass counter and shelves behind it, loaded with textiles, and over it all was a stale smell of sandalwood and incense. A bony flat-faced Japanese opened the door in back, stared at them for a moment and said, "Excuse, please. Be right back," and disappeared again. Bob pointed to the bolts of silk on the shelves.

"You may find something here," he said. "I don't know. There was a little man here who tried to sell me shirts this morning. I might buy some shirts myself now."

Then the Japanese was back, smiling and speaking in a loud guttural voice.

"They have got the most awful voices," Bob said to Mrs. Kingman.

"What you want, ah, please?" the Japanese was saying.

"Lounging pajamas, beach pajamas," Bob said.

"Missy wants them," and he turned to Mrs. Kingman.

"Yes," Mrs. Kingman said, "an embroidered coat and trousers, Chinese embroidery, like that one over there."

The storekeeper gave a polite and happy hiss.

"If don't fit we fix in ah one hour for missy," he said. "Beautiful silk, lovely sewing. Everything very lovely."

"Haven't you got a man here," Bob asked, "named — what's his name?" And he drew the card from his inside pocket. "Oh, yes, Moto."

Now that the door of the shop was closed, shutting out all the sounds from the street, his voice sounded unusually loud and all the shop seemed smaller. The bony shopkeeper glanced sideways from the shelves.

"Mr. Moto," he said, "oh, yes, Mr. Moto busy now. So sorry."

Mrs. Kingman had been looking through a heap of embroidered Chinese jackets and now she lifted one up — blue silk richly embroidered with blues and black and white. She held it up in front of her.

"How does this look?" she asked, and it looked very well with her black hair and her dark eyes and her red lips.

"It looks fine," Bob said, "but then I say — you can wear anything."

"I wish there were a mirror," Mrs. Kingman said.

45

"It's rather large, isn't it? And the trousers are perfectly enormous."

The shopkeeper hissed politely.

"We fix, we fix for missy in one hour," he said. "If lady would like to go in back, very nice ladies' dressing room upstairs — looking glass — everything for ladies."

"All right," Mrs. Kingman said. "I'd like to try it on. You don't mind waiting, do you?"

The shopkeeper opened the door in back and called out something in Japanese and a slight, pale boy appeared.

"He show you," the shopkeeper said. "Very nice ladies' room, up one flight," and Mrs. Kingman followed the boy through the black shadows of the doorway, and the shopkeeper closed the door carefully.

"You say you want shirts?" he said. "Very nice shirts," and he began lifting them down from the shelves, talking in the same loud voice.

"All sewed right here. Everything here we make."

"Yes," Bob said, "I suppose there's a whole nest of you working upstairs in back. Have you got a silk coat to fit me and some ties?"

"Oh, yes," said the Japanese, "very nice coats, very nice ties."

He was reaching for the rack of ties when a sound

from behind the closed door made Bob Bolles look up.

"What's that?" he asked, and the shopkeeper moved toward the rear door.

"Nothing," the man said, "I hear nothing."

"I thought — " Bob said, and then he listened and he heard it again. He was sure of it this time. Behind the closed door he heard a woman scream.

There was something so completely unexpected about it that he must have stood there frozen for a moment, and then he plunged toward the rear door. The shopkeeper stood in front of it.

"Please," he said, "against orders to go up there."

Then Bob grabbed him by the shoulder and flung him away so hard that the man crashed against the shelves of silks. Then he snatched the door open and found himself running up a black narrow flight of stairs.

"What is it?" he called. "What is it, Mrs. Kingman?"

The whole place had a musty, spicy smell that he had once associated with Japanese trains and railway stations. He heard a scuffling of footsteps and voices above him, and then he was on a landing, turning the knob of a flimsy little door. It opened into a room lighted by two windows, obviously a fitting room with a mirror and a chair and a table. And there was Mrs. Kingman. Her shoulders were bare. She was clasping her dress in front of her, facing three chattering Japanese.

"Look here," Bob said. "What's the matter? Did you scream?" Something must have happened. He was sure of it, because her eyes were wide and staring and her face was ashy white. He pushed his way through the Japanese boys and walked toward her.

"Why, Mrs. Kingman," he said, "what is it?" She opened her mouth and closed it. Something had frightened her, something had frightened her terribly.

"I never thought — " she said, but her voice was hardly more than a whisper.

"It's all right," Bob told her. "What happened? Did any of these boys — "

Then her voice was louder.

"Take me out of here," she said, "take me out!"

"Why, yes," Bob told her, "of course I will. It's all right. Just tell me what happened."

She drew a deep breath and her voice was steadier.

"They all came in," she said. "I think they were going to — " She stopped and stared at the door.

"Going to what?" Bob asked her. "It's all right, Mrs. Kingman."

"Going to kill me," she said. "But — " and then her words were steadier, "but it's all right now. Just take me away."

"Oh, come now," Bob said. "Something just startled you," and he turned to the boys and scowled at them. "You boys get out of here! What the hell do you mean breaking into this room?" None of them answered. They only stood staring at him with wooden, vacant faces, and he heard Mrs. Kingman draw in her breath sharply.

"It's all right now," she said again. "Just take me out."

Then Bob Bolles heard quick, light footsteps on the landing, and he saw the man he had seen earlier that morning in his neat white business suit. It was Mr. Moto.

The light from the window glittered from Mr. Moto's glasses. There was something birdlike in the way that Mr. Moto turned his head, first toward Mrs. Kingman and then back toward Bob Bolles, but aside from that quick motion, everything else about him was very tranquil. As he stood with his delicate hands clasped in front of him, he looked patient and reassuring.

It was only afterwards that Bob Bolles wondered where Mr. Moto had been and why he had not appeared sooner. He must have been somewhere near, for he was not out of breath; he showed no signs of hurry.

"Oh," said Mr. Moto, "what is it, please?" And he

spoke to the boys sharply in Japanese. "Was something wrong, please?"

"Look here," Bob said. "Something happened to this lady when she was trying on a dress. I was down in the shop and she screamed."

"Oh," said Mr. Moto, "oh, so sorry. I know now. A misunderstanding, please. Those boys they work so hard. They came to fit the clothes. So very stupid of them. So sorry. They do not understand the foreigners, the boys," and Mr. Moto rubbed his hands together and bobbed his head. "So very, very sorry for the lady. Excuse it, please. So very sorry."

"I tell you something happened," Bob Bolles said. "What was it, Mrs. Kingman?"

"It's all right now," Mrs. Kingman said. Her dress was on again and the color was back in her cheeks. "They just came in so suddenly, without knocking, all of them at once. It — startled me, up here alone."

Mr. Moto clasped his hands and bowed again.

"It is so very awkward," he said. "I hope so very much the lady will excuse. In Japan it is the other way," and Mr. Moto laughed nervously.

"What's the other way?" Bob asked.

"In Japan, please," Mr. Moto said, "everyone undresses in Japan. No one would mind. These boys did not understand. So sorry."

"That's so," Bob said. "You ought to see them in the

50

railroad trains, Mrs. Kingman. They don't mind what they take off in public. But you'd better teach these boys, Moto."

"Oh, yes," said Mr. Moto, "yes. So sorry for the lady. She may have the dress for nothing if she will make no trouble. So very, very sorry. Madam, please, we will close the door. We will be so very, very careful."

"No," said Mrs. Kingman. "I want to go. Please, Mr. Bolles, don't talk to him. I just want to leave here. I don't want to see their faces. I don't — " and she took his arm. He felt her hand shaking as she held it.

"It's all right, Mrs. Kingman," Bob said. "No one's going to hurt you. Of course we'll get out," and he walked down the stairs with her and through the shop, with Mr. Moto following.

"So sorry," Mr. Moto kept saying. "Will Madam please excuse?"

"I'm awfully sorry you had a fright like that," Bob said. "Of course I can see, up there all alone — "

But he could not be sure that something else had not happened, for out in the street she still clung to his arm. Something had frightened her, and she did not seem like a person who was easily frightened.

"Let's go away," she said. "You'll help me, won't you? Please help me."

"Why, of course," Bob said. "I guess I'd better take you back to Mr. Kingman."

Her grasp on his arm grew tighter.

"Oh," she said, "not that, no. Please, listen to me, Mr. Bolles. There isn't much time. I — you'll have to help me."

"Why, yes," said Bob, "of course. Just forget what happened up there. It was really a misunderstanding. No one can hurt you here possibly."

She gave her head an impatient shake and then she dropped his arm. His words must have reassured her somehow. At any rate she seemed to have recovered.

"You've been awfully nice," she said. Her voice was suddenly warm and friendly. "When you came running up those stairs — I should have known that you'd be nice."

"Why, that's all right," Bob answered. "It wasn't anything."

"You'd say just that, of course," she said, "because you're nice. I'm afraid you think I'm an awful fool, going to pieces like that."

"It's all over now," Bob said. "We'll find Mr. Kingman and then you can forget about it."

"But why are you in such a hurry to find him?" she asked, and she smiled at him in a way that made him feel very peculiar. "Girls aren't always tied to husbands. I think he's going to be busy for quite a while. There's no hurry, is there? Just suppose that he weren't here at all."

"What?" Bob asked her.

She looked up at him, half questioningly, half laughingly, so that he could not tell whether she was serious or not.

"Just suppose he weren't here at all," she said. "Just suppose that you and I had met somewhere and that neither of us cared much about convention or anything. I don't, and I don't believe you do."

When Bob looked back at her he knew that it was true — he did not care much about convention.

"All right," he said, and somehow her eyes made his voice unsteady. "Suppose he weren't. He's probably still down there talking at Henry's."

"Just suppose we'd known each other for a little while longer," she said. "Suppose we'd talked about a lot of things and suppose we'd danced together. Suppose I told you that I was sick and tired of everything."

"I've been told that before," Bob said, and he was thinking about the times he had been told, but no one who had told him looked like Mrs. Kingman.

"Suppose we liked each other. We might, you know," she said.

"That's true," Bob answered, and he did not mind at all dealing with the supposition. "We might have once — when I was in the Service, maybe — but I'm an ex-Naval officer now and I'm pretty nearly on the beach," and he laughed.

"I know," she said. "We heard about you from Henry. You see, I'm not very happy and you're not very happy, don't you see? And I suppose there are times when you don't care much what people say. That's why I say — just suppose — "

"Suppose what?" Bob asked.

"That I told you I was in a great deal of trouble." Her eyes were on him, half serious and half questioning. "And that I wanted you to take me away on your boat — anywhere to get away from here. I wonder if you'd do it."

"You'd have to be in an awful lot of trouble to ask me that," Bob said.

"I suppose so," she answered, "but I'm not so sure — if we'd only known each other longer. I wonder if you would. Would you?"

The strange thing about it was that she spoke as though the question were serious, as though there were actually something between them; and he could almost wish there were.

"If you put it that way, I might," he said, and Mrs. Kingman laughed, but somehow she was still half serious.

"Suppose we went right now, right down to the water, and rowed out to your boat, me with nothing but what I have — just this handbag and this dress — and suppose you just pulled up the anchor and hoisted up a sail. We'd be a long way off before anyone knew, wouldn't we?"

"Yes," Bob said, "we might be," and then he laughed. "But you see, there's Mr. Kingman. That's the trouble with supposing."

"Oh," said Mrs. Kingman, "but just suppose — I have plenty of money. I'm quite rich, really."

Bob Bolles felt his face grow red again. That talk of money was the first thing that put him in his place.

"You don't do things like that for money," he said. "At least, I don't," and then he laughed again. "We'd better go and find Mr. Kingman. It's getting late. I imagine he's still down at Henry's. He had to see someone there."

Then he heard Mrs. Kingman catch her breath sharply.

"He had to see someone?" she repeated. "Who?" And Bob's mind went back to noon at Henry's when he had been sitting in the shady barroom — and all the make-believe was gone.

"A new arrival," Bob said, "just off the plane, nice-looking, rather tall, rather young. He said that he particularly wanted to see Mr. Kingman. It was the first time I heard your name and Henry gave him a room upstairs."

Mrs. Kingman grasped his arm again and her voice was very sharp.

55

"Did you hear his name?" she asked.

"Why, yes, I did," Bob answered. "He said he came from Portugal. His name was Durant. Why, what's the matter?"

A spasm of sickness seemed to have struck her. For a second her eyes were half closed and her body swayed against him, and then she steadied herself and stood quite still.

"It's nothing," she said. "It's so hot — the sun — Mr. Bolles — "

"Yes?" he said.

"Will you take me on your boat? Will you right away?"

They had come to a standstill on the corner, near one of the white banks on the square, and all the slow life of Kingston was moving past them unheeded. A truckload of bananas passed them on its way to the pier from some estate in the back country. A group of Negroes walked by aimlessly. Two spruce-looking businessmen emerged from the bank and passed them, without giving them a look. All life passed them by while they stood there. Bob Bolles seemed to be conscious of her for the first time. It was the first time that Mrs. Kingman was not a polite abstraction, but instead a definite person who had become suddenly a part of his life.

"Do you really know what you're talking about?" he asked.

And he could almost believe she knew. She stood there — lithe and straight and tall. The curve of her lips, the curve of her chin, the steadiness of her eyes all told him something. It was more than an impulse with her. It was more considered than that. She half smiled at him, making him look at her, making him see that she was desirable, and all the time she was trying to read everything about him, because something must have made her desperate.

"Yes," she said, "I really know."

She might regret it later, but she was telling the truth. Something had made her desperate — not afraid, but desperate. It was a desperation which had made her toss aside every little conventional concealment. She was nothing but a human being — no longer fashionable, no longer calm.

"You'd better tell me what it's all about," Bob said, and her answer came promptly, almost breathlessly.

"There isn't any time to talk now. It's just you and me — you and me. I'll tell you when we get aboard your boat."

"Well — " Bob Bolles began, but he never finished. Mr. Kingman came around the corner by the bank, walking very fast. He saw them and waved his hand and hurried toward them. She must have seen him at the same instant and her whole manner changed.

"Why, Mac," Bob heard her say, "there you are!"

Although Bob could not define it, there was some-

57

thing a little ugly about it, something surgical and cruel in Mr. Kingman's smile, something very wary in his eyes.

"Hello," he said to her and his glance never left her face. "I thought you were shopping, Helen."

"We were," Mrs. Kingman said. "I was just going to get a — a taxi to go back to the hotel."

"No, you weren't," Mr. Kingman said. "You were talking. I've told you, my dear, it isn't good for you to excite yourself by talking."

"I think Mrs. Kingman is a little upset," Bob Bolles said. From their faces it seemed to him necessary to make some sort of explanation. Mr. Kingman's eyes were icily cool. He was giving every word a complete and flattering attention.

"Upset?" he asked briskly. "How?"

"It was just a little matter in the Japanese store," Bob said. "She will tell you. It wasn't anything, really."

"The Japanese store?" Mr. Kingman said. His voice was light and humorous, but there was no humor in his eyes. "You shouldn't have gone without me, my dear. Don't be afraid. I'll see it doesn't happen again. Nothing will trouble you again, because I'll be with you — always."

"Yes, Mac," Mrs. Kingman said. "Don't be silly."

"I shall not be, my dear," Mr. Kingman said, and

his eyes were back on Bob Bolles. "I should have told you, Skipper, that Mrs. Kingman isn't very well. I hope there wasn't anything that puzzled you. She didn't possibly suggest that you might run away with her?"

"Why, no," Bob said, "of course not, Mr. Kingman."

"Because if she ever does," Mr. Kingman said, "don't take it seriously. Helen's a charming girl, but she's here for a little rest." His arm shot out suddenly and his fingers grasped Mrs. Kingman's elbow. "We really have a — a jolly time together, don't we, dear? We'll get one of those cars over there and go back to the hotel." But Mrs. Kingman did not move.

"Mac," she said, "you've seen Charles?" Mr. Kingman's fingers were still on her elbow, gripping her very hard.

"What?" he began. "What the devil do you know about Charles?"

"Don't lie to me, Mac," Mrs. Kingman said. "Charles called to see you at that saloon and you've been talking to him. Where is he now? What have you done to him?"

Mr. Kingman beckoned to a driver in a car across the square.

"My dear," he said, "we will talk about it quietly in just a minute. And no emotion now, please. You

59

must excuse her, Mr. Bolles. She'll be better at five. You'll see. Say good-by to Mr. Bolles, dear."

"Don't," Mrs. Kingman said. "You hurt me, Mac." Mr. Kingman's hand dropped from her elbow. "Oh," he said, "so sorry, dear. See you later, Skipper." And then Mrs. Kingman smiled at Bob Bolles as though nothing had happened at all.

"Good-by, Mr. Bolles," she said. "Thank you very much."

The touring car and the driver were at the curb and Mr. Kingman helped her in.

"Careful," Bob heard him say, "careful, Helen." And then they were gone and Bob Bolles was left standing at the corner.

"Now, what do you know about that!" Bob Bolles said.

Perhaps Mr. Kingman had been right. Perhaps she was upset and tired. He had seen other married couples — He shrugged his heavy shoulders.

"Maybe it's just as well," he said softly, "that I never married, but it's certainly taken me out of myself."

CHAPTER IV

HE must have stood there for quite a while, thinking of everything that had happened, and it had certainly taken him out of himself. Mrs. Kingman had made him forget his own problems almost entirely. He had almost forgotten that he was standing on the corner by the bank, when he heard a voice behind him calling, "Bob — Bob Bolles!" It was like a voice in his own thoughts when he heard it, for no one in Kingston knew him well enough to call his name, but he understood when he turned — and all his old life was back. He had forgotten the destroyer that he had seen entering the harbor, and now he saw a young officer in starched, fresh whites. It was a long jump from Mrs. Kingman when he saw him. It was Bill Howe, whom he remembered very well at Hampton Roads. He was a junior lieutenant now, and of course he would be assigned to the *Smedley*.

"Hello. How are you, Bob?" he said. "Captain Burke's at the hotel. He sent me to find you."

Bob Bolles felt his face flush.

"What's the Captain doing on the *Smedley?*" he asked.

"Flagship of the division," the Lieutenant answered. "Captain Burke wants to see you."

"How the devil did he know I was here?" Bob asked.

"You know, we talk about you quite a lot," the Lieutenant said. "They said at Key West that you'd bought the *Thistlewood* and the Captain picked her out when we came in this morning. He sent me to find you, Bob. It's orders."

"Well, that was damned thoughtful of him," Bob Bolles said. He paused and looked up and down the street, at the coffee-colored policemen, at the fat old women with their shells and baskets, at the tropical trees in the square and at the automobiles and the hack horses. "You can give Captain Burke my regards and tell him I'm not forgetting that he sat on the Board that passed me over."

The Lieutenant looked hurt. Anything that either of them might say would only make it worse and Bob did not want to explain his feelings to someone who was younger than he, who had looked up to him once and who had listened to his advice.

"It wasn't the Captain's fault he was on the Board," Bill Howe said. "He said he's got to see you. You're just acting childish, Bob."

62

That last remark made Bob Bolles angry.

"I'll act the way I damned please," he said. "All right. Come on."

They began walking up the street past the shops again.

"Bob," Bill Howe began, "you shouldn't take it this way. The Captain thinks a lot of you. He says so."

"For God's sake," Bob Bolles said, "shut up!"

The boy was hurt, but he shut up. It was all a good deal worse than Bob had thought it would be. Everything that he was trying to forget came back. He felt exactly as he had when they had told him he had been passed over. He felt the same anger and the same bitterness. Burke had not been his commanding officer, but Burke had been on the Board.

Harry Burke was in a bedroom on the third floor of the hotel. His coat was off and he was lounging in an armchair with a tall lime-juice drink in front of him. He looked about the same as he had when Bob Bolles had seen him last — forty-five, with gray in his hair, thin and acid and leathery. He stood up and held out his hand.

"So you found him, did you, Howe?" he said. "Bob, it's nice to see you." Bob Bolles did not answer and he did not shake hands.

"You'd better go, Howe," the Captain said, and

neither of them spoke until the door closed. "I never thought you couldn't take it, Bob," he said.

Bob drew in his breath sharply. It did not help to realize that he was making a fool of himself when he had intended to be calm and casual.

"Let's skip how I act," he said. "You went into that with charts and numbers, didn't you?"

"All right," the Captain answered. If he had gotten mad it would have been better, but he did not get mad. "How about a drink?"

"I don't rank enough," Bob said, "to drink with you. What did you want me for?"

Captain Burke sat down again and waved to another chair.

"Listen, Bob," he said. "I wish you wouldn't take it personally. Everybody's name comes up. I couldn't help being on the selection board. You didn't seem to make much of a hit with one of your last C.O.'s and we couldn't disregard the way he rated you."

"Look here," Bob said. "I won the Schiff Trophy. Didn't that make any difference? It was personal prejudice and you know it."

"Maybe it was," Burke answered. "They couldn't select you on your record, but you needn't have got mad. You should have waited. The next selection board might have been entirely different. You knew it would consist of an entirely new group of officers.

Look what happened to Spike Jones last year. He was selected after a 'pass-over.' Plenty are, you know."

"It was personal prejudice," Bob said again. "I've been trying to forget it. Let's skip it."

He saw Harry Burke still looking cool and friendly, and what was worse, he knew that Burke felt sorry for him.

"You don't look as though you had done much of a job forgetting it," Burke said.

"If this is all you want to see me about," Bob said, "I'm going."

But he knew he was not going to go. Now that he was there he would have to go through with it.

"That isn't why I wanted to see you," Captain Burke said. "What good has it done, spending all that money on a schooner and bumming around in it? Now, wait a minute. Sit down. Don't take it personally, Bob. A lot of other good boys missed out on their half stripe. One of your commanding officers gave you a two-point five in co-operation, but he thought you were a damned good flyer. If you hadn't written out your resignation — "

"If I were a 'yes man' I'd have got a four," Bob said. "Is there any good reason why I should sit here — "

"The reason is it will do you good to hear some common sense," Captain Burke told him. "That particular commanding officer had some reasons for what he gave you. There was the time when you took that plane to call on that girl in Baltimore. And there was the time at Kelly's in Panama during the maneuvers."

"My C.O. didn't give me a chance," Bob said.

"You could have a chance now," the Captain answered. "If you went up to Washington — "

"Thanks," Bob told him. "Why should I go to Washington? I was perfectly right and you know it."

There was a moment's silence and Captain Burke sat looking at him, and Bob Bolles looked out the window toward the harbor.

"Bob," Harry Burke said, "you shouldn't have thrown it all away, without waiting for another selection board."

Perhaps he was right, but it was finished.

"I'm glad to be out of it," Bob said.

"Listen, Bob," Captain Burke asked. "How would you like it if you were with me? On the *Smedley* for a couple of weeks?"

He thought he had put it all away from him, but he knew he hadn't as soon as Harry Burke asked him that question.

He had tried to tell himself a good many times that it had not been as bad as a court-martial. Yet in a way it was worse than that, because being passed over for promotion had been a reflection on his personality. It made him doubt himself and it made him hate to see anyone whom he had ever known.

"Do you know what the C.O. said?" Bob asked. "In his opinion my attitude made me unfitted to carry out any mission. How would you like to have that stamped on you?"

"Listen, Bob," Captain Burke said. "That's water over the dam." He had the same look that other friends had worn when Bob Bolles had talked to them — the embarrassed look of people who do not want to listen.

Bob Bolles did not answer.

"Well," he said finally, "don't be sorry for me. I can't take that, Harry."

"How about coming aboard?" Captain Burke asked again. "A couple of weeks on the *Smedley*?"

"What's the idea?" Bob Bolles asked. "How does a civilian rate that?"

"They say you've been cruising around the Caribbean quite a bit," Harry Burke said. "That's so, isn't it?"

"Yes, that's so," Bob Bolles answered. "Since I bought the schooner I've been aboard her nearly all the time. I know every rum joint in the Caribbean — Guiana, Trinidad, La Guayra. I've put the *Thistlewood* into a lot of funny places — just to get away from myself. It doesn't work. You can't."

Harry Burke's manner was suddenly brisk and cheerful.

"Well, you're just what we want," he said. "I'll take you on as a pilot. I have Naval Intelligence Authorization. It's just what I've been telling Welles."

"Who's Welles?" Bob Bolles asked.

Captain Burke looked up at the ceiling.

"Intelligence," he said. "He's with us on this trip. We're on a sort of wild goose chase, looking for something. I told Welles you might have some ideas."

"What are you looking for?" Bob Bolles asked. "Or is it confidential?"

"It's confidential," Harry Burke answered, "but I can tell you some of it. While you've been out here have you ever heard of the *Aquitane,* a French merchant vessel, five thousand tons, Captain LeBœuf, Commander?"

Bob Bolles remembered the *Aquitane*.

"If you're looking for her, Harry," he said, "you'd better learn deep diving. She was down here taking on cargo at Guadeloupe, but they sank her last June off the Bay of Biscay. You don't mean to say they don't know that in Washington?"

"They're not as bad as that up there," Harry Burke said, and he smiled. "There's a rumor — it may not mean anything, but it's important enough to have Intelligence down here with us — there's a rumor that two of the crew were picked up and brought to Brest. Intelligence got their story through the British. Le-Bœuf was carrying something — something he had taken aboard in New York."

"You know," Bob Bolles said, "cargo ships usually do."

"Not always something that worries Washington," Harry Burke answered. "This was for the French Government. LeBœuf was down here when he got the news that the whole business in France had collapsed. The story is that he left what he was carrying down here somewhere, because he didn't want the Nazis to get it. Now the word is the Nazis know it too and they're looking for the crate."

"Crate?" Bob Bolles repeated.

Harry Burke pursed his lips together as though he had tasted something sour. He was clearly trying to decide how far he could go in explaining a confidential mission.

"Suppose it was a knocked-down plane," he said. The Captain's face was wrinkled and careful.

"I didn't know," Bob Bolles told him, "you were so short of planes back home."

He sat there wondering what the Captain would answer.

"It isn't the plane as much as a part of it," Harry Burke said. "If it's at the bottom of the sea that's all right. It's a gadget we don't want used by anybody else. Just one was turned out as a sample. France had an interest. It doesn't matter what it is, except that it's important."

"Not the bomb sight?" Bob Bolles asked.

The Captain shook his head.

"Never mind what it is, as long as you know it's important. I'd like you to come along."

"Why?" Bob Bolles asked.

"Well — " Harry Burke looked at his glass, but he did not touch it, and then he looked back at Bob Bolles. "If the *Aquitane* dropped that plane off it wasn't at one of the regular ports, or we'd have known about it. If it's anywhere it's been left at some out-of-the-way place, some old harbor."

Bob Bolles did not answer. The Captain, sitting there in his clean white uniform, reminded him of what he had lost, and he was filled again with his old resentment.

"It'll do you good," Burke was saying. "It's time you got hold of yourself."

Slowly Bob Bolles pushed himself out of his chair and stood up.

"So you're trying to give me a hand, are you?" he asked. "Thanks. I don't need it."

"Now wait a minute, Bob," Harry Burke began.

"It's nice of you," Bob said, "thinking this up for me, but I can worry along by myself. You can get along without me all right and you know you can." He put his hands in his pockets and smiled. "Besides, I've got business. The *Thistlewood* was chartered for a month this morning. We're leaving this afternoon."

Captain Burke loosened his coat collar with his forefinger and pushed his head forward.

"You mean right this morning somebody wanted to charter that schooner of yours?"

"Yes," Bob answered, "right this morning. It was quite a lucky break. The cops had just asked me to leave."

"Yes," Harry Burke said, "I'd heard about that."

"Well, you needn't worry about it," Bob said. "I'm all right. Don't have me on your mind."

"What sort of a party is it?" Harry Burke asked. "What did they want with you?"

Bob Bolles laughed.

"Nothing to worry you or your Mr. Welles of the Intelligence," he said. "A couple from New York, a lawyer and his wife, both a little nervous, just down here for a rest."

The sharpness left the Captain's face and he looked at Bob again as he had before, in an embarrassed, friendly way, and then he stood up too.

"Whoever they are, I wish you'd walk out on them. Let them relax with someone else. You could be a big help to us. It's time you saw some friends."

Bob felt hot and uncomfortable. He had never

71

realized how through he was, how definitely everything was finished.

"Captain," he said, "it doesn't work. I wouldn't ship with you as an outsider for a million dollars. Just get it into your head that it's good-by to all that. Incidentally, there's quite a lot in the world besides the Navy. Well, so long."

"Bob," Harry Burke said, "haven't you got any sense? What's the use of your making a mess of your life? It's about time you straightened out, Bob. I wish you could look at yourself in a mirror."

"I did," Bob Bolles answered, "right this morning." Then he lost control of his voice. "God almighty, are you trying to put me on the carpet?"

"Quite a picture, isn't it?" said Harry Burke. "You taking out a sailing party?"

Bob Bolles turned on his heel and opened the door.

"Wait a minute," Harry Burke called. "Come back, Bob."

Bob closed the door behind him and walked down the hall toward the stairs. If you started out in one direction you had to keep right on. Yet when he closed the door he had a feeling that he had closed it on the last chance he would ever know. He had the feeling of being completely without a country, entirely by himself. His familiar feeling of doubt was eating at him again and what he needed was a drink.

He walked past the desk, hoping that the clerk was not looking at him. He walked so fast that he almost ran into a small man near the door. It was the Japanese he had seen that morning.

"Why," Bob said, "I'm sorry. I didn't see you, Mr. Moto."

Mr. Moto stepped aside and bowed.

"Thank you," he said. "So very careless of me too, Mr. Bolles."

"Selling shirts to the guests?" Bob Bolles asked.

"Oh, yes," said Mr. Moto, "oh, yes, shirts."

CHAPTER V

THERE were moments when Bob Bolles wondered why he had bought the *Thistlewood,* but he had never regretted the impulse. He had bought her in Florida, from the former owner, after a hurricane had ripped her from her moorings and had smashed her on a breakwater. With the help of a yard owner he had towed her ashore and had made a great many of the repairs himself. Even so, nearly all his savings had been consumed in making the *Thistlewood* fit for sea again. Five minutes after he had bought her and had passed through the first excitement of ownership he realized that she was too big for him. She had been built for ocean races with a skipper and a crew of three or four, and she had carried a lot of sail. Since he could never have afforded such a luxury as man power, he had used all his ingenuity to fix her so that two men might handle her, and the job on the whole had been satisfactory. It was true that her new rigging looked clumsy and her masts too short, but even in rough weather it was possible to manage with the assistance of one other able hand. For almost two years he had lived upon the *Thistlewood,* and he was proud that she was shipshape, no matter how she might look.

When a boatman from the public pier rowed him out to her that afternoon Bob Bolles felt as he often did — that he might have gone clean to pieces if it had not been for the *Thistlewood.*

Her hull, as she lay there in the blue water, was light and graceful. Tom had already got the sails up without his help. They looked small for her size as they slatted idly in the gentle breeze. He paid the boatman and climbed into the roomy, comfortable cockpit and looked forward over the cabin skylight to the open hatch of what had been the crew's quarters. The cabin doors were open and he walked down the steps into the cabin's musty shadow. Mattresses and pillows had grown dingy like all the other furnishings so that the cabin had assumed the air of an apartment occupied by a decayed gentleman, but it was all neat and shipshape. The galley with its little stove near the stateroom was stocked with canned goods. All his belongings had been removed from the stateroom so that it was fresh and neat, with its berth newly made and its little porthole half open. Tom must have worked hard to have got everything ready. Tom was busy forward, arranging a bunk opposite his own.

Bob's clothes were still in disorder on the vacant bunk above it, his oilskins, rubber boots, and rifles. He told Tom to leave it, that they could fix it later, and they went up into the bows and took a few turns on the capstan and got the cover off the jib. They stowed away a tarpaulin and looked at the sail locker.

"We'll check the provisions," Bob said.

He had left with Henry a standard list of necessities, but Mr. Kingman had evidently elaborated on it. He had added whisky, four cases of wine and all sorts of expensive canned goods.

"They're not taking any chances," Bob said, "in case they want to cross the ocean."

He was busy for almost an hour going over everything, not such a difficult job, since he had always prided himself on keeping the *Thistlewood* ready for sea.

"Tom," he asked, "why did you take my guns forward?"

"I just thought you might like them, sar," Tom said, "with strangers aboard."

Tom was always suspicious. He had never liked strangers on the *Thistlewood*.

"Now, listen," Bob told him. "This is just a lady and a gentleman from New York and their valet. Oh, well, all right. Leave the guns there."

Five minutes later Tom called that a boat was coming and Bob came out of the cabin to watch it. A long white launch was moving across the harbor. He could see a pile of boxes and suitcases and the boatman and four people in the stern. One of them was Henry. He saw Mrs. Kingman with a blue scarf around her hat and Mr. Kingman and a short squat man who would be the valet. They were alongside a minute later, climbing up the little ladder into the cockpit. Henry came first, then Mr. Kingman, then Mrs. Kingman.

"Greetings, Skipper," Mr. Kingman said. He looked at the sails and at the boom moving lazily above his head. "Here we are. Are you ready to push — shove off?"

Clearly he was unfamiliar with the sea.

"We can get under way any time you want," Bob said, "as soon as we get your gear aboard. Hello, Mrs. Kingman."

He held out his hand to her to help her aboard. She laid her hand in his and gripped his hand firmly but not too firmly. All he could see in her was a pleased anticipation of a new adventure, nothing more, and she seemed to have forgotten everything else. She seemed to have forgotten what she had asked him, or at any rate she did not want to bring it up. Still holding his hand, she jumped lightly into the cockpit, with a quick little laugh, but he saw her look at Mr. Kingman before she spoke.

"Oh," Mrs. Kingman said, "what a lovely little ship!"

It was obvious that she did not know much about the water either; but it was different with Oscar.

"This is Oscar," Mr. Kingman said, "from Sweden."

A short stocky man in a badly fitting brownish suit stepped into the cockpit. He was carrying two suitcases which must have been very heavy, because his shoulders bent under the weight. He set them down carefully and straightened his broad back and stood with his stocky legs apart looking up at Bob.

"Hello, Oscar," Bob said. "Glad to see you."

Oscar bobbed his head and raised a stubby forefinger to the brim of his cap. His thick right wrist showed a blue tattooed rope, twisted into a lovers' knot. He certainly did not look like a valet. His eyes were a muddy slaty color. His eyebrows and his stubby hair were a pale bleached yellow. His jaw was square, his mouth was large and his lips were heavy, and the bridge of his nose was broken.

"You look handy on a boat," Bob said.

"Yes," Oscar said, "that is right."

His voice was rumbling and guttural.

"Oh, yes," Mrs. Kingman said. "Oscar's been with us for years. Oscar knows about everything, don't you, Oscar?" Oscar grinned and showed a set of teeth too symmetrical to be real, and as an afterthought touched the brim of his hat again.

"I tank so," Oscar said. "Yes, madam."

"Get those bags into the cabin," Mr. Kingman said. "Step — step on it, Oscar."

"Here," Bob called, "Tom, give him a hand."

"Oh," said Mr. Kingman, "no, no, not that. Oscar understands the baggage." He stopped and watched Oscar move slowly into the cabin. "Oscar's quite a character. He can help you. We all want to lend — lend a hand."

"Oh," Bob said, "that's fine."

Oscar was back in a second, pulling out more bags from the launch. The Kingmans had a lot of baggage — bulky canvas cases, steamer trunks, and the kind of cases that could contain the tripods for a motion-picture outfit.

"It's all right," Mr. Kingman said, as he saw Bob watching the growing pile in the cockpit. "Oscar knows where it all goes — camping supplies, guns and what not."

"There won't be any big game," Bob said.

"Sometimes," Mr. Kingman answered, "I shoot at bottles. Let Mr. Bolles take you down, dear, and show you your quarters."

Bob took her below while they continued getting the luggage aboard.

"How wonderfully it all fits together," she said after he had shown her the stateroom and the galley and the folding table. "It's perfect," but she was looking at him and not the cabin. "Mr. Bolles —"

"Yes?" he said.

He thought she was going to say something more, but a footstep on the stairway stopped her. It was Mr. Kingman.

"Here we are," Mr. Kingman said, "and we're going to take your orders, Skipper. You call me Mac and I'll call you Bob. It's easier, what? And I meant to tell you Oscar can handle the cooking."

"That's fine," Bob said. "It might be more comfortable if Oscar bunked forward with Tom and me."

"Oh, no, no," Mr. Kingman answered. "Oscar's nervous if he's away from us."

Bob left them in the cabin. Henry stood in the cockpit, looking toward the shore. Oscar was in the motorboat, wrestling with the last of the luggage.

But for some reason Henry did not look entirely happy. His face, always yellowish and pale, looked paler than usual. He kept moving his hands in and out of his pockets. He seemed very anxious to be back on the launch and leaving.

"What's the matter?" Bob asked. "Have you eaten something, Henry?" Henry's smile was rather sickly.

"Oh, no," Henry answered. "It is only that I have

a good deal of business today. You'll like the King-mans. They're really splendid people."

"Where did they get Oscar?" Bob asked.

"Oscar?" Henry said. "Oh, yes. Well, Mr. Kingman is so lovely to everybody. Oh, there you are, Mr. Kingman."

Mr. Kingman was out of the cabin again. It seemed to Bob that Mr. Kingman was very restless and everywhere at once.

"We won't keep you any longer," he said to Henry. "Everything's all — straight, isn't it?"

Before Henry spoke he seemed to swallow a lump in his throat.

"I think so, yes," he said.

"It can't go wrong, you know," Mr. Kingman said. "Just do what I told you."

"Yes," Henry said.

"Well, don't be so damned fidgety," Mr. Kingman said. "It's perfectly simple."

"I'm not fidgety," Henry said. "Good-by, sir. Pleasant trip."

The launch drew away from the *Thistlewood's* side, and Mr. Kingman glanced astern at the shore. The town of Kingston shimmered in the sun and the high green mountains towered behind it. The natives were still loading bananas. You could hear them calling across the water.

81

"Let's go," Mr. Kingman said. "There's nothing to keep us, is there?"

"Come on, Tom," Bob called. "We'll get the hook up."

"I help him," Oscar said. "Stand by the wheel, sir."

Oscar climbed out of the cockpit and scuttled forward over the deck.

"Well," Bob said, "it's great to have another hand." He trimmed in the mainsheet.

"All clear, sar," he heard Tom call. The jib was filling. Tom was running to the foresheet. The *Thistlewood* was moving. Mr. and Mrs. Kingman stood beside Bob, looking astern. It seemed to him from the tense look on their faces that they almost expected that someone would call to them from the shore.

"Well," Bob said, "you haven't forgotten anything, have you?"

"No," Mr. Kingman answered, "certainly not. What makes you ask?"

"I just saw you looking ashore," Bob answered. "It is a pretty harbor."

Mr. Kingman put his hand above his eyes and still stared at the shore.

"My dear," he said, "we'd better go and set things to rights, I think."

Mr. Kingman, Mrs. Kingman and Oscar were down

in the cabin for a long while with the doors closed, putting things to rights. Standing by the wheel, in the light fair breeze, Bob Bolles could hear their voices, gentle and muffled, but they did not disturb his own thoughts. Leaving a port made him feel that he might be breaking into something new. The sense of anticipation was milder, but it was the same sort which he had always felt just before taking off in a plane, whenever he waited, listening to the roar of the motors. That feeling of moving away from land, that sound of the water on the bow were not bad substitutes. He was going out again, off where no one could help him much but himself.

They were out of the harbor now and the sun was growing low. The mountains of Jamaica were turning already, with the distance, from green to blue. In the morning you might imagine that they had never existed. Already the whole world was narrowing down to the deck and the spars of the *Thistlewood* and the people on the *Thistlewood* would make that world.

Tom stepped into the cockpit noiselessly on his broad bare feet and began coiling the halyards. Now they were at sea Tom looked graceful, almost beautiful. He said it was lovely weather.

"Yes," Bob said, "everything looks fine."

Tom flexed his arm and looked at his muscles.

"That man, Oscar, by Godfrey, sar, that Oscar he is strong."

"Yes," Bob said, "he looks husky."

"By Godfrey, he fished the anchor aboard with one hand, sar."

Bob looked at the compass without answering.

"What they doing down there," Tom asked, "with everything closed up?"

"Settling in, I guess," Bob said. The motion of the *Thistlewood* was increasing and the wind was rising slightly. Tom looked up at the clear sky and grinned. The low sun made his shadow fall across the cockpit in a huge grotesque black shape.

"What's the joke?" Bob asked.

"Just thinking, sar," Tom answered. "Japanese are comical."

"Who?" Bob asked. "What Japanese?"

"That man you speak with this morning, sar. He was out this afternoon in a little rowboat. He come alongside and said everything was so nice — asking where we were going."

"Well," Bob said, "you couldn't tell him, because you didn't know."

Then there was a noise astern. It was the hum of an airplane motor coming toward them and he could see the ship a thousand feet up perhaps. He could see the gray spread of wings and the pontoons underneath.

From the sound he could even tell the make of the motor. It was one of those passenger planes which had done a good trade with tourists a year ago. The roar of the motor grew louder.

"Damn fools," Bob said.

Then just as he spoke the cabin door burst open.

Mr. Kingman bounded into the cockpit with Oscar at his heels.

"Here," Mr. Kingman shouted, "what's that?" From the way both he and Oscar looked you might have thought they had never seen a plane before.

"Here," Mr. Kingman shouted again. He had to shout because the plane was swooping over them. "What plane is that?"

"Just some fool tourist," Bob shouted, "out to see the sunset. Look! She's turning now."

He was right. The plane was banking at about five hundred feet, and now she was going back toward land. The sound of her motor was already dying out.

"Oh," Mr. Kingman asked, "do they do that often?"

"Yes," Bob said. "Two pounds for twenty minutes. They dive down over boats to please the customers."

"Oh," Mr. Kingman said, "just a tourist plane."

"Naturally," Bob said, and he laughed. "You didn't think it was a bill collector, did you, Mr. Kingman?"

Mr. Kingman laughed too and put his hands in his trousers pockets.

"The last touch of land," he said. "Oscar, you mix a — a cocktail for Mr. Bolles and me, and you'd better start with supper. You'll mess with us in the cabin, Mr. Bolles, and Oscar will bring your man something forward."

"Thanks," Bob answered, "if it's convenient."

"We'll have some Rüdesheimer 1934, unless you've a feeling against Rhine wine on account of the unpleasantness. Look at the sun how it drops."

The sky was already a deep purple and it would soon be black. When Oscar came up with a tray and a cocktail shaker and two glasses it was already hard to see Mr. Kingman's face.

"A wonderful moment," Mr. Kingman said. "Will you have another touch?"

"No, thanks," Bob answered. "I don't drink much when I'm sailing," and he raised his voice. "Tom, the running lights."

"Oh," Mr. Kingman said, "must we have lights?"

"Even a small boat carries them at night," Bob said, and he leaned down to light the little lamp in the binnacle.

Anything that morning which had disturbed him about the Kingmans, anything odd in the overtones of their conversation, anything that had even seemed like a strained relationship, was entirely gone at dinner. Mrs. Kingman seemed to be perfectly happy, perfectly content, and all the hardness had gone out of Mr. Kingman's eyes whenever he glanced at her across the table. There was a clean white tablecloth and the napkins were folded to look like little ships. There was turtle soup and roast chicken and a soufflé afterwards. It was amazing that anyone who looked like Oscar could cook so well, and Mrs. Kingman explained that Oscar had set the table and had folded the napkins too. They talked mostly about trivial things, such as their trip from New York. They both seemed pleased with everything and that made Bob Bolles pleased.

"We might play three-handed," Mr. Kingman said, "if you play bridge. Nothing like cards to keep your mind off your troubles, is there, my dear? Let's get the cards — for just one rubber. By Jove, isn't it peaceful? I feel I'm going to sleep tonight, and dream of lonely islands in the sea."

Mrs. Kingman found a pack of cards and shuffled them.

"Cutthroat bridge," she said. "I love it," and she smiled at Mr. Kingman.

That was the only moment when there was the slightest discord, and Bob Bolles never thought of it till much later. It was only later that he remembered that Mrs. Kingman's words had come a little slowly and that Mr. Kingman had raised his head quickly, as though he were listening for something.

"Yes," Mr. Kingman said, "I know you love it, but

be careful with me, Helen. I always hold the cards, and if I don't" — Mr. Kingman picked up his hand and laughed — "I always get them from the dummy. Dummy — that's a funny word, isn't it, Skipper?"

"How do you mean?" Bob asked. "I never thought of it."

"So dead," said Mr. Kingman, "so completely dead."

Mrs. Kingman sighed.

"Don't be so gruesome, Mac," she said. "We'll all be dying sometime."

There was something acid in that passage, but not enough to notice. Bob enjoyed playing bridge with the Kingmans, because neither of them made mistakes.

Tom woke him at two in the morning for his watch.

"A fine clear night, sar," Tom said, "a steady breeze."

The stars were out. The running lights and the binnacle light were surrounded by a yellow glow which ebbed away in the darkness. The sea was dark and rolling and the breeze so steady that it would have been safe to lash the wheel and to have left her on her course. It was a time when you could not get away from yourself — standing by the wheel. First Bob Bolles thought of home, and that was quite a distance away, and then he thought of Bill Howe and of the destroyer in the harbor.

"Oh, well," he said, "oh, well."

There was one thing he was proud of. He was able to look at what he had been and what he was without much emotion. He could stand there at the wheel of the *Thistlewood* and bring back names and faces and events without any particular regret, just as though they belonged in the life of someone else. He could remember when he played football. He was a good athlete in those days and not a bad sort of person. They had liked him in the Service. There had never been any trouble about too few friends.

"It was all too easy," he said out loud, "a lot too easy."

There was no answer except the sound of the wind. There was never any answer for anything, except inside yourself perhaps. Now if he had gone on with engineering and design, it might have been better, but it still might have been too easy. He thought of other men he knew who had started out well and had just burned out.

He could see it all as though it had happened years and years before, because everything smoothed out when the *Thistlewood* put to sea. He remembered the way the sun beat down on the lawn by the officers' quarters and the way the motors sounded on the field that morning when he heard how the Board had passed on him.

"I'm sorry you take it that way," the C.O. had said.

Of course he wasn't sorry, really, and there had been no other way to take it.

"You'd better think it over and reconsider," the C.O. had said.

"No, I'm getting out, sir," Bob Bolles had told him, and of course the C.O. had the last word. The superior officers always did in the Service. . . .

"*Come on,*" Bob said. "*Stop thinking.*"

All of him was back in the cockpit of the *Thistlewood* again. He was back again, going through the motions.

Then the door of the cabin opened. There was no particular reason why it should have surprised him, except that he had thought of himself as entirely alone.

"Why, hello," he said. "Can't you sleep?"

It was Mrs. Kingman with her white coat wrapped around her. Even when she walked toward him her face was vague and blurred.

"No," she answered. "I was awake. I wanted to see the water. We're so near it, aren't we? I've never been so near."

"Yes," he said, "we're near to it." She moved near to him, so near that he could see the light from the binnacle reflected in her eyes. He was intensely, almost insistently, aware that they were alone and he knew that she had not come out to see the water, and he suddenly knew that he had been hoping that she might come out and speak to him. All the time that he had been thinking about himself he had been thinking about her too.

CHAPTER VI

SHE sat down near the wheel, so near that she could speak very softly, and he saw her glance toward the closed door of the cabin.

"I think he's asleep," she said, "but I'm not sure. You don't mind my being here?"

"No," Bob answered, "only —"

"Never mind about Mac just now," she said. "I couldn't sleep. That's all. You must think I'm an awful fool."

"Why?" he asked.

"From what I said to you. You'll forget it, won't you?"

"Why, yes, of course," he said.

"Thanks," she said. "You're awfully nice. Women are very foolish sometimes. Sometimes —"

But she did not go on. Neither of them spoke for quite a while and she sat there looking at the misty whiteness of the sails.

"Do you know what I'm thinking?" she asked him.

"No," he said.

"I'm thinking I wish I'd known you long ago. I was thinking about it in the cabin tonight. When two people meet they feel that way sometimes. You know what I mean, don't you?" Bob Bolles did not answer.

"You don't answer," she said, "because I'm someone else's wife. That's it, isn't it?"

"Yes, that's it," he said.

"But you know what I mean, don't you?"

"Yes," he said, "but it doesn't do any good. It would be much better — "

"That's it," she said. "You're awfully nice. But I'm glad you know what I mean. I've heard about things like this happening. If we'd only known each other long ago before the war, before everything was all in pieces, we might — "

She stopped as though she wanted him to finish, and he did so, almost before he thought.

"We might have fallen in love," he said.

"Yes," she said. "I'm awfully glad you said it, my dear. We might have — if we'd only met some other time, somewhere else."

"Where?" he asked.

"Oh, anywhere," she said, "anywhere, but here. When I could be myself and you could be yourself. Let's talk about what we used to be."

He could not see her face clearly, but there was a

little catch in her voice, as though she had thought of checking herself before it was too late.

"Haven't you always been what you are now?" he asked.

"Oh, yes," she answered quickly, "of course. I was thinking about you. You used to be in the Navy, didn't you?"

"I'm out of it," he said. "I resigned. I was passed over for promotion."

"But why?" she asked. "Did you do something wrong?"

"My personality and my temperament," he said.

"Oh," she said. "What were you in the Navy?"

"Aviation," he said.

"Oh —" It seemed to him that her voice had changed again. "I didn't know that."

"Does it matter?" he asked her.

"No," she said quickly, "of course not. I just like to know about you. Why were you in the Navy?"

Her questions had been kind and gentle, but her insistence made him restless.

"I wanted to do something for my country," he told her.

Then he wished he had not said it, because it was too naïve to say out loud, too much like the pledge you took when you saluted the flag at school.

"It doesn't sound right, does it?" he asked.

"Oh, yes, it does," she answered. "I think you're

very nice, my dear. I feel a good deal the same way about my country."

She was quiet for a while after that, and he was glad that she was.

"You're not happy, are you?" she asked.

"You mentioned that before," he told her. "You said you weren't. Is anyone?"

"It's silly not to be happy," she answered, "as long as you're alive."

Bob Bolles was thinking that they had covered a lot of ground in that random talk of theirs, and the more she talked the less he could understand her.

"Yes," she said again, "I wish we'd known each other long ago."

"How long ago?" he asked her. "Where did you used to live?"

"Oh," she answered, "nearly everywhere. When I was four or five we lived in one of those big apartment houses on Gracie Square in New York."

"Wait a minute," Bob said. "There weren't any apartment houses on Gracie Square when you were four or five."

She laughed. She seemed to be very much amused.

"I was just trying to see how well you knew New York. Where should I have lived?"

"In the East Sixties," Bob said, "and you should have played in Central Park."

"Well, that's exactly where we did live," she said.

95

"In the East Sixties, near Columbus Circle. The circus used to be near there, at the Garden."

Bob Bolles faced her squarely and tried to read her face in the dark.

"Look here," he said. "Why are you lying to me?"

"Why," she asked, "what do you mean, lying?"

"What I say," he answered. "The Garden was on Madison Square then. Who are you? What's the matter? You'd better tell me."

"Why —" she began, but he stopped her.

"Who are you?" he asked her again. "You've come up here to try to find out who I am. What was the matter today? What are you frightened of?"

"Stop!" she said, and her voice was very low. "I'm getting cold. I'm going now."

"Who are you?" he asked her again. "You'd better tell me."

"No," she answered, "please, my dear, don't ask me. But I want to tell you something and it's the truth." She paused and glanced at the cabin door, and then she put her hand over his.

"I didn't come here to get anything out of you. Don't think that, please. I'm worried about you, very worried."

"Why?" he asked.

"Because I like you. I really do. Everything I said was true. It wasn't a lie. You must promise me something."

96

"What?" he asked her.

"If anything should happen," her voice was very low and insistent, "about Mac or me — don't ask me what I mean — you mustn't interfere. You mustn't ask questions and you must keep out of it. Do you understand?"

"Why, for heaven's sake?" Bob asked her. "What might happen?"

"It hasn't anything to do with you," she answered. "Don't ask. Just keep out of it."

"Now, wait a minute — " Bob Bolles began, and then she snatched her hand away from his. The cabin door was opening.

"Oh," she said, "is that you, Mac?" And Bob saw Mr. Kingman's head and shoulders in the cabin doorway and Mr. Kingman climbed quickly up to the cockpit.

"My dear," he asked her, "how long have you been here?"

"Not long," she answered, "just for a few minutes."

Mr. Kingman put his hand on her shoulder and she stood up.

"Not exchanging confidences with the Skipper, were you?" He spoke gently, but there was something icy in his question.

"Not exactly confidences," Bob Bolles said easily. "We were just talking about when Mrs. Kingman was a little girl."

Mr. Kingman laughed and pushed her gently toward the open cabin door.

"You mustn't mind her, Skipper," he said. "Helen's a great one for talking. I hope she didn't disturb you. It's bad for you to be out in the night air, my dear. You mustn't do it again."

"Mac," said Mrs. Kingman, "I just wanted to find out —"

"To find out," Mr. Kingman said. "Come down to the cabin, dear. Good night, Bob."

It was a long while later — the sky was growing a little lighter than the water — when he saw Tom walking over the deck to relieve him at the wheel. He could always count on Tom to wake up without assistance when his watch came around.

"Keep her as she is," he said, and Tom took the wheel.

"Yes, sar," Tom said, "as she is," and he pointed toward the cabin. "Are they all sleeping down there, sar?"

"Yes," Bob said. "Why shouldn't they be?"

"Sar," Tom said, "I think they do act queer."

"Listen, boy," Bob said. "All rich people act queer."

"Someone go on tippy-toe," Tom said, "tippy-toe. Someone try the door up forward."

"What?" Bob asked. "In the forward bulkhead?"

"Yes, sar."

"You've got great ears," Bob said. "Forget it, boy. Maybe it was Oscar being lonely."

"Yes, sar," Tom said. "I think they want to kill us, sar."

For a moment Bob Bolles was so surprised that he did not answer. Then he gave Tom a sharp cuff.

"Don't be a crazy nigger," he said. "Call me if you want me."

He went forward, crawled into his bunk and lay staring at the beams above him, listening to the sound of the water close to his ear. That last idea of Tom's made an odd climax to the whole day. He would have thought it amusing if it had not exasperated him. He was thinking that no white man could ever tell just what went through a Negro's mind. . . .

CHAPTER VII

A SHARP unfamiliar sound awakened Bob Bolles and pushed him into a sitting posture so suddenly that he had struck his head smartly upon the berth above him. The sun was coming through the open hatch. His oilskins were swaying on the hook by his bunk. He could tell from the sun that it was quite late in the morning. Tom must have let him sleep through a watch, as Tom did sometimes. Then he heard the sound again — the sharp report of a high-powered rifle — and he was on his feet almost without thinking, running up the ladder. The sweetish salt air of the Caribbean struck his face and he saw Tom standing at the wheel grinning. Mr. Kingman, dressed in orange-colored slacks and a striped shirt, was standing balancing a rifle, looking out to windward. Oscar in faded dungarees with his shirt open at the throat was holding an empty bottle and Mrs. Kingman in gray slacks and an olive-green shirt with little gray sailboats on it, bare-headed and with sun glasses, stood just behind him. As he watched, Oscar's heavy arm moved in an arc and he threw the empty bottle. It fell splashing on a blue wave, far out to windward, and Mr. Kingman raised his rifle and fired. *Crack,* it went; *crack, crack.*

"Ah," Mr. Kingman said. "Throw another, Oscar," and then he saw Bob Bolles climbing down into the cockpit.

It is not an easy thing to hit a bottle from a small boat with a rifle. Mr. Kingman certainly knew how to shoot. The whole scene was careless and pleasant. Mrs. Kingman smiled at him, but he could not see what her eyes were like behind the glasses.

"It's Mac's hobby," she said.

Mr. Kingman handed the rifle to Oscar.

"Take it away and bring up Mr. Bolles's breakfast. By Jove, this is the — the life, isn't it?"

Oscar brought up folding chairs and set up a table. All their clothes, all the equipment were like numbers in a sporting catalogue. Tom went forward and Bob took the wheel again while Oscar brought him orange juice and bacon and toast.

"You'd think that with those big hands of his that Oscar might be clumsy," Mrs. Kingman said, "but he isn't. Do you know what he's doing already? He's making a little ship to go in a whisky bottle."

Oscar grinned, but he made no comment.

"When you get it finished," Mrs. Kingman said, "you'll give it to Mr. Bolles, won't you, Oscar?"

Oscar's mild blue eyes moved down from the luff of the mainsail, stared at Bob for a moment and turned to Mrs. Kingman.

"Huh?" he said.

For some reason it seemed to Bob that Oscar's monosyllable was disturbing. He saw Mr. Kingman glance toward Mrs. Kingman sharply, as though he wanted to stop her, but Mrs. Kingman went right on.

"You will give it to him, won't you, Oscar?"

Oscar gave the wheel a little tug and something working in his mind seemed to amuse him.

"Ay tank so," he said, "if he should need a little ship in a bottle." Mr. Kingman moved impatiently.

"That is about enough from you, Oscar," he said.

"If Oscar's such an old sea dog," Bob asked, "why didn't you charter a boat without a master?"

Mr. Kingman had been gripping the arms of his chair, half leaning forward to listen, but now he relaxed.

"Oscar can't navigate," he answered. "And speaking of navigating, how about getting up the chart?"

"I'll fetch the instrument up too," Bob said. "I'm going to shoot the sun at noon."

"Oh," said Mrs. Kingman, "shoot the sun."

The cabin was more spick-and-span than he had

ever seen it. When he opened the locker and took out his chart book and instruments, he could hear their voices outside.

"From now on," he heard Mr. Kingman say, "you keep your face shut, Oscar."

When he was up on deck again and had opened the chart on the folding table Mr. Kingman rose and leaned over, looking at it eagerly.

"Where are we now?" he asked.

"About here," Bob said. "I'll tell you accurately at noon."

"Oh," Mr. Kingman said, "I see our line. We're already quite a way from everything."

"Yes," Bob said. "It's a pretty lonely sea."

Mr. Kingman pointed farther down the page.

"And those dots — those are the islands there?"

Bob Bolles nodded.

"Those islands, have you anything that shows them larger?"

Bob turned the pages of the big book until he came to the plate marked "Winderly Group" and there they were.

"The big one is Mercator," he said.

Mr. and Mrs. Kingman crowded close to the table.

"That looks like a harbor," Mr. Kingman's voice sounded sharper. "Could a ship, an ocean liner, get in there?"

"Not enough water," Bob said, "too much reef. You can see the figures."

"Those other two islands — what are their names?" Mr. Kingman asked.

He was pointing at two other bits of land which lay perhaps forty miles to the westward.

"Jacks Island," Bob Bolles said, "and St. Edith."

"Could an ocean liner touch at either of them?" Mr. Kingman asked.

Bob Bolles looked up from the chart.

"Not enough water," he said, "too much reef. But a ship with a light draught like this one can anchor in that bay at Mercator, though it looks like a tricky passage."

But Mr. Kingman's mind was still back with the ocean liner.

"I suppose," he said slowly, "a big vessel could stand offshore and send in a small boat, couldn't she?"

"Why, yes," Bob said, "of course. Do you know of a boat's calling there, Mr. Kingman?"

"Know of some boat?" Mr. Kingman said slowly.

"Mac," Mrs. Kingman said, "Mac."

Her voice made Bob look up from the chart. Something had made her face strained and white. Oscar was still holding the wheel, but he had moved in front of it.

"No," Mr. Kingman said, "do not bother, Oscar.

104

What do you mean, Bob, I should know of some boat?"

"What's the matter?" Bob asked. "I didn't mean anything." That was the first time his mind had moved, putting things together. Mr. Kingman laughed.

"Of course you didn't, Bob," he said.

The *Thistlewood* was moving through fine weather, pushed on by a brisk fair breeze so steady that you hardly had to trim a jib from one day to the next.

All the first day out Mr. Kingman kept looking astern or going to the bow with his glasses, as though he expected to see something, but at the end of that time he gave it up. And there was nothing worth watching, except now and then a line of porpoises breaking the water and diving in unison, or the flying fish that darted off the bow and whizzed in a straight line through the air and popped into the sea again.

"They look as if they had been wound up with a key," Mrs. Kingman said.

The sea, Bob thought, was doing both Mr. and Mrs. Kingman good. Their faces had looked drawn and tired in Kingston, but now the lines had gone out of them. They shot at bottles sometimes or took sun baths or dozed on deck and every evening they asked Bob Bolles for dinner and bridge in the cabin. Sometimes it seemed to him that they were like himself, glad to forget who they were or where they were going, for they did not talk about their background any more than he did. They lived entirely in the present, and even Oscar grew mellow and agreeable.

Just as Mrs. Kingman had said, Oscar had the most amazing way of making things. He had picked up all those little skills which you associate with an old seaman who has been in sail. He finished his little ship with all her masts and yards laid flat and then he thrust it into the neck of a bottle and pulled a bit of silk thread and up came the masts and spars with all their standing rigging.

That idea of Tom's about murder and sudden death often amused Bob Bolles. He even asked Tom about it the third night out when Tom awakened him for his trick at the wheel.

"Anybody tried to kill you yet?" Bob asked, as he pulled on his sweater.

"No, sar," Tom answered. "But what for Mr. Kingman keep looking all the time," Tom asked, "like he's afraid someone is after him?"

"Rubbish," Bob Bolles said.

"And wherefor," Tom asked, "should Mrs. Kingman be afraid of him?"

"Afraid of him?"

"Yes, sar," Tom said. "She makes eyes at him, afraid, when she talks to you, sar" — but she never talked to Bob alone again until the last night out.

The breeze seemed to be dying down that night, although they were making five knots when he had looked at the log. Standing alone in the cockpit, he kept turning his head so that the wind would strike his face. There was no doubt that the wind was dropping. By morning there might be a flat calm or a change of weather, but judging by the barometer and by his instinct he felt that the weather was going to hold. Nevertheless, the wind had shifted a point or two. He went forward and trimmed the jib and the mainsheet a trifle. When he came back a figure was standing near the wheel, and he saw that it was Mrs. Kingman.

"I shouldn't be up here," she said. "I can only stay a minute." Her words were quick and a little breathless. "He's asleep, but you can't be sure."

"Look here," Bob Bolles began. Nothing had seemed out of the ordinary for days until she appeared. "I've been hoping for a chance to talk to you. What's so mysterious now? What is it?"

"Don't," she said, "don't talk so loud. 'He's so — so jealous. He's a very queer man, very — but don't mind that. How far are we from land?"

The binnacle struck her face as she stood near him by the wheel. Her face looked drawn and pale.

"I don't know exactly," he told her. "There's always a certain element of gamble in trying to hit a little spot like Mercator on the nose. It's easier to navigate a plane than a small boat, I think." She did not answer and he went on. "If you want my guess, from the way the clouds looked at sunset and from the way the air feels, we should see something of the Winderly Group at dawn, probably the hill at Mercator."

"Then it's over," she said, "and we've hardly seen each other at all, have we?"

"Do you mind?" he asked her.

"Yes," she said, "I do. Do you?"

It wasn't right — talking to her so — and in the end it added up to nothing.

"Yes," he said, "I don't understand you. You're like — "

"Like what?" she asked.

"Like a frightened lady in the dark," he said. Her lips were half open and then she closed them and shook her head.

"You're wrong there," she said. "I'm never very much afraid. There was a moment in Kingston, when I screamed, but never mind about that."

"I've got eyes, you know," Bob said. "There's Mr. Kingman."

"Are you jealous of him?" she asked him. "You don't have to be."

"I didn't mean that," Bob answered. "You're afraid of Mr. Kingman, aren't you?"

She gave him a strange, quick look and shook her head.

"Don't say that," she said. "I hate it. I'm not afraid for myself, only for you."

"Never mind about me," Bob answered. "I can look out for myself, I guess. If you're not afraid of him, you don't trust him, do you? This isn't just a vacation on a boat, is it? I'm not a fool. There's something else."

"Yes," she said softly, "there's something else."

"Then, you'd better tell me," Bob said. "I'd be glad to help you."

He thought that she hesitated for a moment. She seemed to be weighing his offer very carefully, and then she shook her head and smiled at him.

"No, my dear," she said. "I've thought of it. It isn't your cup of tea." He started to speak, but she stopped him.

"No," she said, "don't interrupt me. You must understand this. You must. No matter what happens, it isn't for you. You're not the kind. That's why I like you. It may be very dangerous and I can't say too much. He — he won't stop at anything. I wish you'd understand."

"Then, you are afraid of him," Bob said. "Who is he? What are you doing here anyway?"

"Please don't ask," she answered quickly. "You mustn't ask. Perhaps I can tell you sometime, but not now. I suppose I'm a fool. I want to try to help you." She stopped, but she went on before he could speak.

"It's awful to be a woman. To be lonely — always lonely. You may hate me before this is over, but please, please, don't do anything. You can't understand. You're an American. I'm French. What — " She stopped again. "What are you looking at?"

"I can't make you out," Bob said. "I wish — " And then he glanced astern and rubbed the back of his hand across his eyes. "I wish I knew what you're talking about."

"What are you looking at?" she asked.

"I thought I saw a light," Bob said. "Yes, there it is." Her hand fell on his arm and gripped it tight.

"I don't see anything," she told him. "Where?"

It was away off in the dark. It would bob up and disappear again, but he saw it distinctly a moment later.

"It looks like the light on the mast of a motor cruiser," he said. "What do you suppose she's doing out here? She's on our course. She's coming nearer."

"Are you sure?" she asked him.

"Reasonably sure," he said. "Why, what's the matter now?"

Something was the matter, because she ran away from him and yanked open the cabin door.

"Mac," she called, "Mac! There's a boat coming up behind us."

There was a scuffling noise in the cabin and then Mr. Kingman came running up the steps.

"Oscar," he called, "come on, Oscar! You say there's a boat? Where is it, Bob?"

"Look out," Bob said. "Don't barge into me like that."

But Oscar did not answer. He and Mr. Kingman were staring at the light.

It was easier to see now. It was clearly a motor cruiser, coming fast. He could see the light on the mast and the green and red running lights. Mr. Kingman was standing absolutely motionless.

"By God," he said, "it is coming! Oscar, go down and fetch the Brenn gun. No, wait a minute. Go forward and put out our lights."

"Here," Bob Bolles said. "You and Oscar can leave my lights alone."

It was just as though he had not spoken.

"Go ahead, Oscar," Mr. Kingman said, and Oscar jumped into the cockpit. Bob Bolles dropped the wheel and stepped in front of him. He was angry, perhaps unreasonably angry.

"You stay where you are," he said, and he saw Oscar, a vague white shape, lunge toward him.

"All right," he heard Mr. Kingman say. "Go on, Oscar."

Oscar was close enough so that he could see him more clearly by then. Bob took a quick step backwards, found his balance and drove his right fist with all his weight behind it straight to Oscar's face. He heard Oscar give a grunt and he knew that he had hurt him and he knew that it was better not to stop with that, now that he had started. He stepped in with his left, and then he sent in his right again, and he was lucky, because he must have caught Oscar on the jaw. Oscar sank down on his knees and put his hands in front of him, sprawling on all fours just above the hatch that housed the auxiliary engine. The *Thistlewood* had come into the wind and the boom bounced just above his head and the sails were making a roaring, snapping sound. Mr. Kingman was standing just in front of him. Mr. Kingman's voice was very steady. All the excitement seemed to have left it.

"You should not have done that," he said. "I think — "

"Mac," he heard Mrs. Kingman say sharply, "Mac! If we can see their lights they can see ours."

Mr. Kingman turned his head slowly.

"Helen," he said, "perhaps you'd better go into the cabin."

"No," she said, and her voice was quiet and very

urgent. "Mac, stop that — and remember — *Suppose what we want isn't there.*"

"Oh," Mr. Kingman said, "oh, yes. Awfully sorry, Bob." His voice had changed suddenly. It was warm and friendly. "Of course you are quite right, Skipper." He leaned down and slapped Oscar hard on the back. "All right, Oscar. Forget it."

"I don't know what the devil's the matter with you," Bob said. "But this is my ship. See?"

He had to speak loudly because of the slatting of the sails.

"Can you stop that noise, please?" Mr. Kingman said. "It's all right, Oscar. Go and fetch the Brenn."

Bob took the wheel again. The sails filled. The *Thistlewood* was back on her course. Oscar was on his feet, shaking his head.

"Fetch it up here. You — do you hear me?" Mr. Kingman said, and Oscar moved toward the cabin.

"Do you think that boat's going to come aboard us?" Bob Bolles asked. "Is that your trouble, Kingman?"

He was over being angry. He could even feel the contagion of Mr. Kingman's excitement, now that the lights were coming nearer.

"Yes," Mr. Kingman said, "exactly that."

"Well, she isn't," Bob said. "She's a half mile to starboard of us and she's keeping on her course."

"Oh," Mr. Kingman said. "Yes, I see." And he raised his voice: "Never mind, Oscar."

From the lights she was a big cabin cruiser and she passed them as though they were standing still. It was a long while before Mr. Kingman looked away from the lights.

"Well," he said, "she cannot be looking for us. What's she doing here, do you think, Bob? Is she on her way to Mercator?"

"No," Bob answered, and he meant it. "Nothing goes to Mercator. She'll be going south — Trinidad, perhaps."

Mr. Kingman stood silently thinking and no one said a word until he spoke again.

"If she stops at Mercator, of course we shall see her in the harbor."

"That will be the only place for her," Bob said, "but nothing stops at Mercator."

"We must be ready," Mr. Kingman said, "just in case. Call me if you see her lights again."

"Maybe it would be easier," Bob told him, "if you'd tell me what your trouble is — not that I give a damn."

Mr. Kingman laughed. Everything seemed better, now that the boat was gone.

"I don't wonder you ask," he said, "not a bit. I'll tell you how it is, Bob. You don't mind my calling you Bob, do you? I wish you'd call me Mac. I keep asking you."

"All right. Go ahead, Mac," Bob said.

"You certainly could handle Oscar," Mr. Kingman said. "That was quite a sight!"

"Go ahead, Mac," Bob Bolles said again.

"All right," Mr. Kingman said. "Let's put it this way. It isn't really anything that need bother you at all. I'm representing a — a shipping company. There was some freight left on — on one of those islands." Bob Bolles felt his hands grip the wheel more tightly, but he did not speak.

"Let's let it go at that," Mr. Kingman said. "I guess you've been around a — a bit, haven't you, Bob?"

"Yes," Bob Bolles said, "quite a bit."

"You're a very — very nice guy," Mr. Kingman said. "How about a drink before we turn in? Oscar, bring us up some whisky."

CHAPTER VIII

A HALF hour later Bob Bolles lashed the wheel and went quietly forward, climbed down the hatch and closed the cover behind him, and lighted the lantern.

"Tom," he whispered, "Tom! Where are my guns?"

Tom pulled himself out of his bunk.

"On the upper berth, sar," Tom said. "Under the blanket yonder, sar."

Bob Bolles ripped the blanket away from the upper berth. There was nothing beneath it — not his rifle, not his shotgun, not his automatic pistol.

"What's the matter, sar?" Tom asked.

Bob Bolles's mouth felt as dry as flannel. A tingling sort of shiver moved up and down his spine, as though something unpleasant were just behind him, but he tried to tell himself that he was not afraid. He had always hated people who got rattled, but still the absence of those firearms of his was an inescapable shock, and all sorts of other impressions of the last days began drifting through his mind.

"Shut up," Bob whispered. "I want to think."

It was no longer a matter of suspicion, for everything in his mind came together — the first glimpse of the Kingmans, what Captain Burke had told him, even the way that Mr. Kingman tripped and hesitated over slang and colloquialisms. He was as convinced as though he had read it on a printed page in daylight that Kingman was looking for the same thing that the *Smedley* was after. Mr. Kingman had found out somehow that it was on Mercator or on one of the Winderly Islands. Mrs. Kingman was in it too, but she was not his wife. She was in that relationship only from expediency. There was nothing that would seem more harmless than a man traveling with his wife.

"Sar," Tom whispered.

"Shut up," Bob Bolles whispered back. "Take it easy, Tom."

He was still trying to work it out. They were traveling together for some purpose of their own, and she had said that she was afraid for him — not for herself. He should have read long ago in Mr. Kingman's eyes that Kingman was a man whom it would be dangerous to run up against — as dangerous as hell. He could see why she had warned him now.

"Mac," Mrs. Kingman had said, "suppose it isn't there."

That had torn it. They were looking for the same thing as the *Smedley*, but they still weren't quite sure where it was. That was what had stopped Kingman — they would need him if what they wanted was not there.

Once — it seemed like a long while ago, although it had not been so long — he had been used to thinking and acting very quickly, for there had been a time when a second's delay might be much too long. He had been taught to estimate a situation and to act. He had been taught that it was better to do something, even if it might be wrong, than to do nothing. After the first shock of surprise the outside circumstances did not particularly disturb him. In fact, he knew already almost instinctively what he was going to do.

What made all his reactions slow was the conflict inside himself. He had been used so long to thinking that nothing mattered — and now he felt alive, so completely alive that he could not believe it. Something was back in him that he had thought had gone out of him for good.

"Please, God," he said softly, "don't let me be wrong. Don't let it all wash out."

He did not realize that he had spoken aloud, until he saw the startled expression on Tom's face. He scowled at Tom and shook his head. He wanted a minute more to think. It was like walking in the dark. As matters stood, both he and Mr. Kingman were walking in the dark. Mr. Kingman didn't know how much he knew and, for himself, Bob didn't know what it was Kingman was after, exactly.

"Listen to me, boy," he whispered to Tom. "You can read, can't you?"

He reached in his bunk for the logbook of the *Thistlewood,* found a pencil and began printing very carefully on one of the back pages.

"Don't talk," he wrote. "When we get into harbor slip overboard and swim to the beach. Go hide in the bush. When everyone is ashore and out of sight swim back and slip the cable. Start the engine and take her offshore. Keep her there until you see a fire on the beach. That's all."

He tore the page from the logbook, handed it to Tom and watched him read it very slowly. Tom was a good boy. He knew that Tom would do it if he could.

"All right," he whispered. "Remember," and he took the paper out of Tom's hand and lighted a match to it.

"I'll take your watch," he said. "That's all."

He had done the best he could. It might not work, and again it might. He went aft again and climbed into the cockpit and took the wheel. The cabin door was closed, but the Kingmans were not asleep. He could hear the low, insistent murmur of their voices. Even through the thickness of the cabin door their voices sounded troubled. Probably no one on the *Thistlewood* would sleep any more that night, and he was not surprised when Mr. Kingman came out of the cabin.

"Hello," he said. "Is that you, Bob? I thought your colored boy was taking over."

"No," Bob said. "Tom's acting sort of queer."

"What's the matter with him?" Mr. Kingman asked.

It was like the beginning of a game between him and Mr. Kingman. They would know each other a good deal better before they each got through.

"You can't ever tell what's going to be the matter with a Negro," Bob said. "That's boy's just gotten moody and he acts scared. Never mind about it. It's going to be light soon. He'll be all right."

"Well, that's fine," Mr. Kingman said. "I've been thinking, Bob, the best thing for us to do — "

Bob Bolles did not answer. In the faint light from the binnacle he could see Mr. Kingman trying to read his face.

"When you went forward after you had that drink what did you go to look for?" Mr. Kingman asked.

Bob Bolles hesitated, and then he told the truth. He

120

was quite sure that Mr. Kingman had known what he had gone to look for.

"My gun," he answered, "but I guess you knew it wasn't there."

Mr. Kingman gave a short good-natured laugh.

"I thought you'd be looking for it. Bob, you and I aren't going to need guns. We can get on hunky — hunky-dory without guns."

"I'm not looking for any trouble," Bob Bolles said.

"I know you're not." Mr. Kingman's voice was warm and cordial. "And there's no reason why there should be any. Of course you know by this time I have a piece of business to do on this island."

"Yes," Bob said, "of course."

"But it needn't make any difference to you," Mr. Kingman said. "If I tell you it's legitimate you'll believe me, won't you?"

"Yes," Bob answered, "that's all right."

"And then suppose," Mr. Kingman said, and his voice was slow and careless, "we just go along the way we have been going, and suppose I give you five thousand dollars, so you won't talk afterwards — one thousand now, four when we get to Kingston. How would you like that, Bob?"

"Fine," Bob Bolles said, "Mr. Kingman."

"Call me Mac," Mr. Kingman said. "I really wish you would. Here — " He pulled a billfold from his pocket. "Here you are. We don't need guns," and he laughed. "We're all clear now, aren't we, all hunky-dory?"

Bob took the bill and put it in his pocket.

"That's mighty nice of you, Mac," he said. "Don't worry about it."

"I'm not," Mr. Kingman said, "not at all. We'll just be one big happy family, won't we, and we'll see land by morning, won't we?"

"Yes, Mac," Bob Bolles said.

"Call me when it's light, will you?" Mr. Kingman asked. "Good night."

Bob Bolles sat down on the transom beside the wheel. Now that Mr. Kingman had gone, he felt very much relieved. He was sure now that Mr. Kingman wanted things to be quiet and he was sure that Mr. Kingman did not know or guess how much he knew.

"Quite a boy," he whispered beneath his breath, "quite a boy."

Light had come quickly on that sea, so quickly that you could almost see it travel across the water. That morning was like the lifting of a curtain and the dawn was so clear and definite that the night seemed hardly possible. In the first gray of dawn Bob Bolles saw that there was land ahead, and the landfall gave him solid satisfaction. First there had been clouds on the horizon and then a darker mass that was black and unsubstantial beneath the clouds. Then as the first shafts of sunlight came over the sea the dark land became faintly green, a small island floating in a misty haze, and the land rose sharply to a hill whose torn, serrated edges, even in the misty sky, showed its volcanic origin. It was like a thousand other islands in that sea, a half-forgotten place, over which the history of the Caribbean would have passed. There would have been the Carib Indians first, and then perhaps a stray Spaniard, and then the buccaneers. After that there would have been the English sugar planters and the slave gangs. He had nearly memorized its nautical description: —

Mercator Island, largest of the Winderly Group, rough and hilly, four miles long and one mile wide, may be distinguished by large V-shaped cleft in long ridge on the center of the island. Volcanic, coral reefs two miles offshore. This island is now inhabited only by two or three Negro fishing families which move to other islands of the group. Harbor only for small vessels, eight feet mean low water. Anchorage in so-called Westerly Bay near remains of coral stone dock. Channel through reef very narrow. . . .

Then there were the bearings, the cleft in the hill, a tall rock on the northwest and the roof of the old planter's house known as Westerly Hall. . . . That was about the way the nautical description went.

"Tom," he called, "get the engine going." It would be safer to go in under power. Tom came aft very quickly and began to pull back the engine hatch and Bob Bolles asked him if he had everything clear. Tom nodded and started to speak.

"Don't talk," Bob said. "Here, take this," and he handed Tom the thousand-dollar bill. He had never realized before how fond he was of Tom and he was very anxious to have Tom entirely out of it.

"Lord almighty — " Tom began.

"Shut up," Bob said, "and remember."

Tom was down by the engine, turning over the flywheel, when Bob knocked on the cabin door.

"Good morning, Mr. Kingman," he called. "We're about five miles off Mercator."

Then a few minutes later everyone was up, and the sun rays broke out of the mist and everything seemed completely fresh and new. He could almost believe that the Kingmans had forgotten everything that had happened in the night. The thing to remember, Bob kept telling himself, was that Mr. Kingman had not the remotest idea of how much he knew or guessed. Mr. Kingman was dressed in a suit of brownish Nanking silk and he was wearing a khaki-colored pith helmet. The clothes made him look cool and competent, like an experienced traveler in the tropics. He was holding an expensive pair of binoculars and he smiled at Bob and called good morning to him and Mrs. Kingman smiled at him too. In her slacks and gay shirt, her sun glasses and her beach hat, she still looked like a picture in a travel folder for a Caribbean cruise. Even Oscar appeared to have forgotten the trouble of the night before. Although one side of his face was swollen, he grinned at Bob Bolles and raised his finger to his forehead. The engine gave a cough and started.

"We'll go in under power," Bob said to Mr. Kingman. "If Oscar wouldn't mind he might help take in the sails. There's Westerly Bay opening up," Bob said. "That's where we're going."

All of Mr. Kingman's attention was given to examining the shore line.

"I see nothing in the bay," Mr. Kingman said, "except one small fishing boat pulled up on the beach. There can't be many people there."

"That's right," Bob said. "I've always heard that Mercator is a very lonely island."

He could almost believe all over again that there was nothing peculiar about the Kingmans.

"Why aren't more people living here?" Mrs. Kingman asked. "It's so green and such a lovely island."

"Twenty, sar," Bob heard Tom call from the bow. He looked carefully at the streaky water ahead and put the helm a little to starboard.

"I've read a little about the history of Mercator," Mr. Kingman said, "if you want to hear it."

"Why, yes," Mrs. Kingman said, "tell us, Mac." And Mr. Kingman told them, while Bob Bolles watched the channel.

"This group, the Winderly Group," Mr. Kingman said, "used to be a stopping place for the buccaneers and pirates. It was very useful for them, because it was so remote, and then in about 1730 two English planters came here from Nevis. Nevis is quite a distance away. They could only rely on themselves for protection and they were burnt out twice by the French. They had to run up into the bush on the hill, but each time they came back, and finally, in about 1770, the island was owned by a planter named Swaith. He was a very able man and the story is that some member of the Swaith family who lives at Nevis now still owns the island — not that it does him any good. The story is that the family moved out for good fifty years ago. You see, there isn't much money in sugar now."

"Swaith," Mrs. Kingman said. "That's a funny name."

"And I guess Swaith was a funny man," Mr. Kingman said, "judging from that book of mine; but he knew how to run a little sugar island. He was rich and he got richer. The story is, when Mr. Swaith was doing well, that he had over a hundred Negro slaves.

He brought artisans over from Nevis who built this house called Westerly Hall and a sugar mill and outbuildings. He cleared the level land by the foot of the hill. He built a dock and warehouses. He even had a small fort on the point. It was a self-contained community — one white planter's family and a lot of slaves."

"What happened to him?" Mrs. Kingman asked.

"It's only another story," Mr. Kingman answered, "of a plantation running down. He died and his son ran it. In 1800 there was an insurrection of the blacks. The Swaiths got away and for a while the island was a small black kingdom. Then there was some pestilence — the smallpox or the plague. Nearly the whole population died and most of those that were left went away. Since then no one has been near it much. The Negroes have never liked it. They've always been afraid of ghosts and now, I suppose, the jungle has come in, but if you look on the hill there you can see a building."

They were near enough by then so that everything was clear. It was a wild bit of land with a rich heavy growth of trees, and brownish cliffs near the water and a white beach bordering the bay with coconut palms near the white sand. There was a silver ribbon of stream falling over rocks near one end of the beach, with rich ferns and plantains growing near its edge, and perhaps a quarter of a mile from the shore were the gray walls and the gaping windows of the ruins of a square stone house, and on a promontory near it you could see the crumbling remains of what appeared to have been a tower.

"There's all that's left of it," Bob said. "That must be the Hall."

It stood there in a tangle of trees, lonely and bleak and sad, and somehow the sight of it gave the white beach and the quiet water a sinister watchful sort of silence. They were through the reef and in the bay now. You could see the palm trees and the tops of the great white-limbed candlewoods waving in the breeze. You could hear the sound of the breakers on the reef above the chugging of the engine.

"What was the tower for?" Mrs. Kingman asked. "Why did they have a tower?"

"It will be one of the old windmills," Bob Bolles said, "for grinding the cane."

He dropped the wheel and reversed the engine.

"Tom," he called, "let her go." There was no answer and he raised his voice.

"Tom, where the devil are you?"

Mr. Kingman turned his head from the shore.

"He is not in the bow," Mr. Kingman said.

Bob Bolles shut off the engine.

"He must be below," he said. "I'll fetch him," and he ran toward the bow.

"Tom," he called, "Tom!" But he knew that Tom was gone. He let go the anchor himself and stood watching while it dropped to the clean sandy bottom. Then he looked down the forward hatch and called Tom's name again.

"The boy's gone," he said. "He must have swum ashore."

Mr. Kingman's pale eyes met his, clear, searching and expressionless.

"That is very funny," he said. "Does your boy do that often?"

"Of course not," Bob answered. "He must be crazy, but I'll get him back all right."

"Yet just why should he have done that?" Mr. Kingman said.

Mr. Kingman stood gazing at Bob with a sort of gullible, wide-eyed innocence and Bob Bolles gazed back at him. That innocence of Mr. Kingman's made Bob wonder whether he had been wrong about everything, until he saw Mr. Kingman's eyes. In spite of Mr. Kingman's bewildered, inefficient expression his eyes were thoughtful and steady. They were the sort of eyes which one associates with a clever and active man and not with a comfortable and tired businessman from New York. While Mr. Kingman waited Bob Bolles tried to make his own face look half puzzled and half irritated. He was doing his best to conceal a sharp elation and he hoped that Mr. Kingman had not seen it, for he understood now that Tom was going to do his best. There was a chance, certainly a chance that Tom would get the *Thistlewood* away, and if Tom did, there would have to be a showdown.

"Never mind about that boy," Bob said. "I told you last night that something was the matter with him. If you want to know the truth, that boy is scared to death."

"Scared?" said Mr. Kingman. "Of what?"

Bob Bolles smiled. He was doing better than he thought he could.

"Tom heard the trouble last night," he said. "He had some fool idea that it wasn't safe for him here. He told me we'd get killed if we stayed aboard."

"Oh," Mr. Kingman said, and he laughed. "Let's forget it then. But — but I hope you don't feel that way, Bob."

And Bob Bolles found himself laughing back.

"I don't," he said. "Don't worry."

"That's — that's bully," Mr. Kingman said. "We're just all one family going ashore for a good time. It's all hunky-dory. Let's get out the little boat. We'll take some food. We may want lunch and, Oscar, let me have my rifle. There might be some — some monkeys in those trees."

Oscar pulled the dinghy alongside and held it while Mr. Kingman climbed in.

"Give Helen a hand, Bob," he said. "Now, my dear . . ." Bob Bolles looked at the supplies in the cockpit.

"You'll have to make two trips," he said. "Let Oscar take some of the dunnage with you. I'll wait till he comes back." Mr. Kingman glanced at him sideways with his rifle cradled in the crook of his arm.

"No, no. You come with us, Bob. Oscar can make a second trip." Then Mr. Kingman laughed as though he had thought of something bizarre and very amusing. "We don't want you to get frightened too, Bob, and take the boat away. That would put us in a — a pickle, wouldn't it?"

Bob climbed into the bow of the dinghy. Mr. Kingman possessed a peculiar sort of gaiety — a *joie de vivre* — that was friendly and appealing; and Bob could not help laughing too.

"I like it," he said. "I don't want to run away."

Oscar took the oars and the dinghy moved steadily toward the beach, propelled by Oscar's short hard strokes.

CHAPTER IX

"It looks very lonely," Bob heard Mr. Kingman say. "I see no one."

It was true. The little half-moon of the beach gave an appearance of complete desertion. The waters of the bay were so still and clear that you could look down and see the fantastic growths of coral and the sea anemones waving their long fingers tirelessly and languidly. Little yellow fishes with black stripes and ruby-red fish were darting back and forth in the shadows of the coral.

"Oh," he heard Mrs. Kingman say, "it's like a glass-bottomed boat!"

Ahead of them the white strip of sand shimmered dazzlingly and behind the beach beneath the coconut palms was a dark green shady tangle of trees and shrubs and vines and it was all so quiet that you could hear the chatter of parrots in the trees. If the land by the beach had ever been cleared the jungle had crept back over it many years ago. If there had been a factory and warehouses from the old sugar days the walls would be half buried under vegetation. Bob Bolles could see some signs of vanished industry as they neared the beach, enough so that he could trace the plan of the old plantation days. Ahead of them was a crumbling pier of coral stone, reduced by the storms and neglect into a mass of rubble, with the end disappearing into the water. He glanced back to Mr. Kingman sitting in the stern.

"You'll scrape the bottom off if you land there," he said. "The beach is easier."

"Yes," Mr. Kingman said, "the beach is easier. I see that little fishing boat, but I see no one. It's lonely as — as hell."

Back from the pier, you could still see an open way through the trees that would have been a wagon road, winding up to the walls and gaping windows of the owner's house on rising ground, perhaps half a mile distant. On the beach near the pier was a small open boat canted on its side and farther back were two huts made of palm leaves.

"There must be people," Bob Bolles heard Mrs. Kingman say. "Why don't they come to meet us?"

Bob turned his head again. Mr. and Mrs. Kingman were seated in the stern. Mr. Kingman held his rifle across his knees, his right hand over the trigger guard. He was looking very intently at the thatched huts and at the dark undergrowth beyond them.

"You can't tell how people will act — the natives here are all Negroes," Bob said. "They've run into the bush, hiding."

"Afraid, are they?" Mr. Kingman asked.

Bob Bolles shook his head.

"Not afraid, just shy. They'll be watching us."

"Yes," said Mr. Kingman, "it is very lonely."

The beach gave you exactly the feeling that comes with any abandoned place where life has once been rich and active. Bob Bolles began to wonder how much of the level upland had been under cultivation and where the warehouses would be and the stables and the mill and the overseer's house and the old slave quarters. They seemed to be all gone, except for that half-wrecked and lonely pier and for the crumbling tower of the windmill and the gaunt and stricken walls of the manor house, but at the same time there was an indefinable sense of where they were, the same sense you might have of a presence in a room when someone has just left it. The memory was still there, not unpleasant, of vanished people and vanished voices. It was as though time had stopped.

Oscar gave a last tug to the oars and the dinghy moved silently toward the beach. For a second before the bow grated on the soft coral sand Bob was keenly aware of the sweetish, musky smell of the tropical vegetation and of the land smells mixing with the soft breeze off the water. He could hear the notes of birds in the woods, harsh and discordant, and the slatting sound of the palms and the soft rustling of the candlewoods behind them. He could hear the sound of a small fresh-water stream pouring over the rocks. No one spoke. They must have all been listening and perhaps they had the same sense he had, that everything was watching and waiting. Then there was a faint shock and a hissing sound as the bow of the dinghy struck the sand. Bob stepped into the water and seized hold of the bow. Oscar splashed into the water too and, without speaking, both of them pulled the dinghy to the dry sand of the beach. Mr. Kingman, looking ahead of him at the shore line, stepped out quickly, still cradling his rifle in the crook of his arm, took a few quick strides across the sand and stopped, looking at the trees. He reminded Bob Bolles of a quail hunter waiting for the birds to rise, but nothing stirred. Bob offered his hand to Mrs. Kingman and she stepped ashore too.

"Oh," she said, "what a beach! See the little shells," and she knelt down to look at them, dozens of shiny brown cowry shells with white spots and spidery snail shells and orange clamshells.

"Never mind them now, my dear," Mr. Kingman said. "It seems that no one's here. We have it to ourselves."

"Oh, people are here all right," Bob answered. "Look at the path down from the huts. There'll be at least two families living there."

"Well," said Mr. Kingman, "let us go and see," and he began walking toward the palm-leaf huts near the pier and Mrs. Kingman followed him and Bob walked behind her and Oscar came last. The huts were in a cleared space under the palms right on the edge of the old road whose remains Bob Bolles had seen from the water, and behind them, smothered by vines, he could see the ruins of a low coral stone building. The roof had fallen in long ago and it was almost obliterated by vegetation.

"One of the old warehouses," Bob said, and then he pointed. "There's a fire burning. There was someone here this morning." Mr. Kingman had seen it too — the smoldering remains of a cooking fire in a little circle of stones in front of one of the huts.

"Hello," Mr. Kingman called. There was no answer. "Hello!" he called again.

There was no answer, but suddenly Mr. Kingman took a quick step forward. He was staring at the side wall of one of the huts.

"By — by Jove, Helen," he said, "look at that, will you! Look!"

Mrs. Kingman looked and Bob Bolles looked too. The front wall of the hut was thatched with the leaves of the coconut palm, but the side wall and the rear wall were constructed from the wood still fresh of a packing case, heavy plywood, roughly sawed and roughly nailed to the framework. Bob could even see the remains of stenciling, and the word FRANCE had been painted on the wood with a black brush.

"Oh," said Mrs. Kingman, "why — "

Mr. Kingman gave a low, excited laugh.

"I think it's here, my dear," he said. "Yes, I think our troubles are nearly over. By Jove, look! There's the name *Aquitane* on it!"

"Yes," said Mrs. Kingman, "it's the packing case."

"You see what it means," Mr. Kingman said. "They broke it out right here on the beach. They carried it farther ashore. It's here. You've led us to it, my dear!"

Bob Bolles could see what he meant. There was no doubt about the plywood and the writing that now formed the side of that native hut, and everything that he had thought was coming closer together. That plywood had once formed the side of a packing case, such as was used for shipping an airplane. He had seen natives use those packing cases in other parts of the world. Anyone could read its story. The *Aquitane,* the French ship which had interested Captain Burke, had anchored off the reef of Mercator Island. A plane had been taken from her and had been placed on shore. The plane had either been uncrated on deck and a part of the crate had drifted in, or it had been uncrated on the beach.

"Well, this fixes it," Mr. Kingman said. "It's stowed away somewhere," and he laughed again, a happy laugh of complete relief.

"Now," he said, "this is certainly my luck. If it's here, naturally we'll find it. The main thing is to — to keep our shirts on, isn't it?" He turned to Mrs. Kingman, still smiling. "We've beaten the Japs, my dear. It will simply be a pleasant walk and a picnic in the country. Oscar can go back and get us a few provisions." He looked up at the palm trees and up toward the house on the hill. "Oscar, you might go back to the boat and get the food and the other rifle, although I can see no trouble."

Except for Mr. Kingman's rifle — and for the familiar way he handled it — and for that occasional hardly noticeable hesitation over words and phrases — Mr. Kingman might still have been an intelligent, good-natured tourist, anxious to get the most out of an unusual and expensive vacation. He was genially at ease while they waited for Oscar to come back from the *Thistlewood,* at ease and in very high spirits. He called Mrs. Kingman's attention to a flight of parrots and he asked Bob Bolles quick and intelligent questions.

"The red earth is volcanic, is it not? And you can

138

see the black, basaltic formation in the mountain. By Jove, think of living here, with bananas right by your door — those are bananas on those great green-leafed trees, aren't they? — and every day like a day in June — 'What is so rare as a day in June?' as Longfellow said. Wasn't it Longfellow, dear?"

"Yes," Mrs. Kingman said, "at least I think so, Mac."

"I can always ask Helen for a quotation when I am wrong," Mr. Kingman said. "It was Longfellow, wasn't it, Bob?"

"No, sir," Bob Bolles said, "it was James Russell Lowell — 'What is so rare as a day in June? Then if ever come perfect days.'"

"Of course," said Mr. Kingman. "Yes, by Jove, Lowell, not Longfellow — Lowell, the — the good gray poet."

Bob could not help being amused, and he could imagine that this was exactly as Mr. Kingman wanted it.

"That was Whitman," Bob said. "He was the good gray poet."

"Why, of course," Mr. Kingman said. "Helen, isn't it — A 1, that we brought Bob along with us? Why, he knows navigation and poetry and about the — the wild flowers. 'Then if ever come perfect days,' and it is a perfect day, although it's November, not June."

"Yes, Mac," Mrs. Kingman said, "it is a perfect day. 'Captain, oh, my captain, the fearful trip is done.' "

"Now, who wrote that one?" Mr. Kingman asked. "Whitman — Robert Louis Stevenson — Swinburne — but never mind it now. You know this is all new to me, and to Helen too. By Jove, it gives you a creepy feeling, doesn't it? The sea, the jungle over everything, and we on the edge of the lost world. What a place it must have been when the plantation was going!"

His voice trailed into silence and he looked around him with a bright, happy smile.

"And now," Mr. Kingman said, "here comes good old Oscar. Help him with the picnic hamper, will you, Bob?"

Oscar was coming up the path from the beach, grunting and puffing beneath a heavy load. He carried a canvas packsack on his back, filled with canned goods and bottles. There was a rifle slung over his shoulder, in one hand he had a heavy suitcase and in the other a picnic hamper.

"Why," Mrs. Kingman said, "Oscar looks like Santa Claus."

"Good old Oscar," said Mr. Kingman, "just like Santa Claus. Not that bag, Bob, the other — the picnic hamper. We'll try the house first." Mr. Kingman peered at Oscar's canvas packsack. "Ah, three bottles of Rüdesheimer. We can cool them in some spring. They may make us sleepy after lunch, but then 'What is so rare as a day in June?' "

They were all in a little group in that clearing near the pier, and Bob Bolles remembered later, when he tried to reconstruct the scene, that Mr. Kingman's eyes had been fixed on the tangled vines and bushes in front of him, until he examined the wine that Oscar was carrying. When he turned to look at the wine bottles his head had moved sideways away from the beginning of the old road which led from the dock. The road was nothing but a grassy trail that wound beneath a gigantic candlewood whose heavy roots ran through the grass like enormous hands. Suddenly Bob Bolles saw Oscar's body stiffen.

"*Achtung*," Oscar said sharply. "*Ach* — " and Bob remembered later that Oscar had never spoken a German word before. Suddenly Oscar was not a Swede but a German. Mr. Kingman whirled about before Oscar could finish and Bob Bolles turned too, moved by that sudden urgency in Oscar's voice. A moment before there had been nothing on the path; but now beneath the cool black shadow of the candlewood, not twenty feet away, a small man in a grass-stained white suit was standing, holding a short blunt automatic pistol.

"Please," he said sharply. "Mr. Kingman, please." His last word ended in a gentle persuasive hiss, and before he spoke Bob Bolles recognized him. It was the Japanese from Kingston — Mr. Moto.

CHAPTER X

THERE was a silence — a strange, shocked, stony silence — and for some reason the opening line of that poem still ran through Bob Bolles's mind: "What is so rare as a day in June?" He was standing just a pace behind Mr. Kingman, so that Mr. Kingman's silk coat, his pith helmet and his shoulders were like the foreground in a picture beyond which were the glade and the candlewood and Mr. Moto. He could see Mr. Kingman's muscles beneath the coat taut and absolutely motionless. Mr. Kingman was holding his rifle ready at his hip, but the line of its slender dark barrel was a little off the mark, although an instantaneous flick of Mr. Kingman's wrist would bring it bearing straight on Mr. Moto's body. An almost imperceptible motion, a pressure on the trigger — and there you were.

Yet Mr. Kingman waited and Bob Bolles knew what he was thinking, as he watched the back of Mr. Kingman's head. He saw a little bead of perspiration roll down Mr. Kingman's neck. He could not see Mr. Kingman's eyes, but he knew that they were boring into Mr. Moto's eyes and Bob knew that any moment something might break that perfect equilibrium of time. Mr. Kingman was standing there, figuring it to a hair's breadth. He was estimating his chances if he moved and fired and Bob Bolles was completely sure that no consideration was disturbing Mr. Kingman, except the possibility of success.

There was no doubt any longer who Mr. Moto was. Mr. Moto was no longer wearing glasses, and somehow he no longer looked like a small man, although he was very small. His delicate body, held so motionless, seemed to be made of springs that might snap at any instant, but his face was almost placid — high cheekbones, narrow jaw and narrow dark eyes which were absolutely still. There was no doubt who any of them were. There was an absolute coldness in their attitude such as Bob Bolles had never seen. They were there to do a piece of work, and nothing would stop them — no scruples, no thought of personal injury. They were carefully trained graduates of the most dangerous school in the world, so well-trained that they could keep their tempers and their wits, so well-trained that they could control every tremor of fear and nervousness. The thing that Bob Bolles remembered best of that moment later was a curious quality of icy calm politeness. He was never able to forget the respect that he felt for all of them, a sort of respect that was almost admiration. Mr. Moto's eyes never moved, but there was no indication from his voice that his life and Mr. Kingman's were both hanging from a single thread.

"Please," Mr. Moto said, "no reason for this now. Later perhaps, but not now, please," and suddenly he smiled. "If we start it will be so very, very difficult. So few of us will be left."

"Oh," Mr. Kingman said, "do you think so?" His voice was unshaken, almost unchanged.

"Oh, yes," Mr. Moto said, "I think so. It is so nice when No. 1 people meet on missions. You and I, we are first-class. We are thinking of the end. I was so relieved when I knew it was you, Mr. Kingman. Please, it is better to wait, for now so few of us might be left that nothing could succeed for any of us."

"Oh," Mr. Kingman asked, "what makes you so sure?"

The gold in Mr. Moto's teeth glittered again.

"There was a combination so very like this in Singapore," he said, "an associate of mine was so impetuous. He shot before he thought. So much better to think."

Mr. Moto paused, but he had not moved his dark narrow eyes from Mr. Kingman's face.

"I have been waiting for some minutes for this chance to talk. I could so very, very easily have shot you from cover, Mr. Kingman; but I think this way is better."

"Oh," Mr. Kingman said, "why is it?"

"I am not an airplane mechanic, Mr. Kingman, and you are," Mr. Moto said. "So much better that we work together."

"Oh," Mr. Kingman said, "so that's it, is it?" But neither of them moved.

"Yes, please," Mr. Moto said. "I should be so sorry. If you move now I think that I should kill you before you have your rifle pointed. In the meanwhile the other man with the bags, he would have a shot at me of course. It is so very dangerous. Do you see? We might be so very much hurt that there might be no result for any of us. So too bad, Mr. Kingman, after so much trouble."

The tension about Mr. Kingman's shoulders relaxed.

"I can see your reasoning," he said. "What do you suggest?"

"That is so nice," Mr. Moto said. "I was so sure it would all be so happy. It would be so much nicer if we could make some arrangement for a little while. I should be so honored to take your word — to do nothing for ten minutes."

"Well," Mr. Kingman said, "all right. There isn't any hurry."

"So nice to be working with nice people," Mr. Moto said.

Mr. Moto put his pistol in his pocket and Mr. Kingman put his rifle in the crook of his arm.

"It was careless of me," Mr. Kingman said. "I should have seen you. I thought I was better in the bush. . . . All right, Oscar. . . . So that was you on the boat last night? She wasn't anchored here."

Mr. Moto took a purple handkerchief from his breast pocket, took off his Panama hat and wiped the band.

"Excuse, please," he said. "So very hot, I think."

Mr. Kingman also took off his sun helmet and mopped his forehead. His eyes were coldly blue, but his voice was unruffled and agreeable.

"I was looking for that confounded motorboat," he said. "You did it very well. I'm not generally so easy to — to get a drop on. I knew you were on the job, of course. You Japs get nearly everywhere these days, don't you? You almost picked Mrs. Kingman off in Kingston too, didn't you? I wasn't quite ready for that either."

Mr. Moto put on his hat again and gave the crown a gentle pat.

"It was an effort, please," he said. "You were recognized when you got off the boat. The English police were quite stupid, I think. But, please, it was not to pick Mrs. Kingman off. Simply to extract the location. We knew she had it, please."

"I see," Mr. Kingman said. "I wonder if you tried the factory in the States."

Mr. Moto nodded.

"Just as you did, Mr. Kingman. It was too well guarded, was it not?"

And then the tenseness was gone, just as though Mr. Moto had flicked it aside with his handkerchief, and Bob Bolles felt his own body relax. Now that it was over, it seemed unbelievable, and yet when it had been happening it had seemed perfectly right and logical. You could not believe such a thing unless you had seen it, and now Mr. Moto was smiling and Mr. Kingman looked frank and guileless. They seemed drawn together in a companionship in which Bob Bolles had no part. Oscar set down the suitcase and hamper. Mrs. Kingman looked pale around the lips, but she did not look surprised.

"Mac," she spoke in a low sharp voice and Mr. Kingman nodded to her.

"It is all right," he said. "Leave this to me."

Mr. Moto walked toward them, fanning himself with his Panama.

"May I introduce myself, please?" Mr. Moto asked. "So much nicer," but Mr. Kingman looked puzzled.

"Have I ever seen you anywhere before?" he asked.

"So sorry," Mr. Moto said, "only for so little time. Ha-ha, the Japanese they look so much alike — Vladivostok, in 1934, and then in '38 in Berlin."

Then Mrs. Kingman spoke again.

"Why, Mac," she said, "that year — what were you doing in Berlin?"

"My dear," Mr. Kingman said gently, "never mind it now." And Mr. Moto bobbed his head.

"I am Mr. Moto," he said. "So very honored to represent the interests of my Government, so glad to be acquainted, Mr. Kingman, and the lady — she is German? So sorry she is here."

"German?" said Mrs. Kingman sharply. "We're French, from the Vichy Government."

"Oh," Mr. Moto said, "I understand. I had always heard that Mr. Kingman worked for himself — not for any government — and then sold. So very businesslike — " and he bowed again, and Bob Bolles found himself wishing that he would not keep bowing. "I am sorry, very, very sorry you are here, Miss — " Mr. Moto paused and waited. "So much better if you had stopped in the silk shop." Mr. Kingman shrugged his shoulders.

"She is Mrs. Kingman — just at present," he said, "and that's my man Oscar working with me, and this is the skipper from my boat," he jerked his head sideways toward Bob Bolles. "Now you've got us straight, if you hadn't before."

149

Mr. Moto was still smiling, but there was no humor in his eyes when he looked at Bob Bolles.

"An American," he said. "Yes, we've met. So very sorry he is here. We are searching for the same thing, of course."

Mr. Kingman's voice was suddenly sharp.

"You haven't found it yet?"

"Not yet," said Mr. Moto gently, "but I am very sure it is here."

"Look here," said Mr. Kingman, "would you mind telling me how you found this island? I thought our information was exclusive."

"Yes," said Mr. Moto, "no reason why I should not tell you. I was sent to watch for you in Kingston after we tried the factory — so unpleasant at the factory. When I saw you take your boat I took a plane and watched your course. When I saw where you were pointed, I was so sure, please, where you were going. There was no plane to charter for the distance, without disturbing the police. I hired a motor cruiser in Kingston. It took me two days. The English are so very suspicious. We landed here early this morning."

Mr. Kingman drummed his fingers softly on his rifle stock.

"Where is the crew now?" he asked.

The smile died out of Mr. Moto's face.

"So sorry," he said. "It was better to send the boat

back. I wanted no inside interference, please. I am a scientist searching for butterflies."

"All right," said Mr. Kingman. "How are you planning to get back?" Mr. Moto looked across the clearing to where the *Thistlewood* lay anchored in the clear blue water and his voice grew more gentle and very patient.

"Please," he said, and his right hand dropped carelessly into the pocket of his soiled, grass-stained white coat. "I shall arrange it later."

Mr. Kingman laughed.

"You don't think I'm going to take you, do you?"

Mr. Moto sighed and shook his head.

"It is what I say," he answered, "this is so very serious. My trouble is that I am not a mechanic, Mr. Kingman. I am hoping so very much that we can work together to find an airplane which the French vessel, the *Aquitane*, left here. Mrs. Kingman, I think, brought you the information it is here. I hope to take from it the important new appliance, and to find from you or Mrs. Kingman exactly what it is."

Bob Bolles rubbed the palms of his hands carefully on the sides of his duck trousers and he felt his heart beating in his throat.

"I see," Mr. Kingman said, "there is only one trouble, Mr. — Mr. Moto."

"Yes," said Mr. Moto, "what is that?"

"I want it myself. I'm on a specialist job — you see."
Mr. Moto shook his head sadly.

"So sorry," he said. "But one of us will have it, Mr. Kingman, in the end."

"And you're here all alone?" Mr. Kingman said. "You — you think you can tackle the whole lot of us?"

"So nice," said Mr. Moto softly, "so nice you understand."

"Well, thanks for telling me," said Mr. Kingman heartily. "You're a damned — damned cool customer." Mr. Moto looked slowly at the four of them, and then his eyes rested on Bob Bolles again.

"I can see," he said to Mr. Kingman, "why you brought the lady, for she no doubt has special information, but for this man who sailed the boat — I do not think it was wise of you. I am surprised to see him here, very much surprised."

They were all looking at him and never in his life had Bob felt so entirely alone. Mr. Kingman was half smiling, half frowning as though the remark annoyed him. Oscar licked his lips as though they were dry, but what alarmed Bob most was Mrs. Kingman. For the first time that morning Mrs. Kingman looked afraid.

"Mac," she said quickly, "you promised me. There isn't any need."

"Of course there isn't," Mr. Kingman said heartily. "Bob here is as right as — as rain, and Bob will back me up. It's four against you, Moto."

Mr. Moto's face was wooden and expressionless. His voice was monotonously precise.

"So sorry," he said. "I think the lady might walk away for a moment. It would be nicer, I think."

"What do you mean?" Mr. Kingman asked. "No need to go, Helen."

"I say again, so sorry," Mr. Moto said. "Do you not know this man is formerly a lieutenant commander in the Navy of the United States?"

"Of course he was," Mr. Kingman said. "I know that, Mr. Moto. And he was — was busted out of it. He's a — a harmless drunk, excuse me, Bob. He's being paid enough so he'll be happy for two years. It's all hunky — hunky-dory."

"What is that word, please?" Mr. Moto asked.

"Hunky-dory," Mr. Kingman said. "American slang. It means everything's all right."

"Thank you," said Mr. Moto. "Your English is so very good, Mr. Kingman. I have studied at an American university and I do not speak so well. I am so sorry."

"For God's sake," said Mr. Kingman, "don't keep on saying you're sorry. You're sorry for what?"

"So sorry for Mr. Bolles," Mr. Moto said. "Excuse

153

me, you were not very careful. Do you know where Mr. Bolles went after you saw him, Mr. Kingman? It is why I am sure it will be so much nicer for us to work together for a little while."

"No," Mr. Kingman said. "Where did he go?"

Mr. Moto rubbed his hands together softly.

"He went," Mr. Moto said, "straight to the hotel. So sorry for you, Mr. Bolles. And there he called on the officer of the United States destroyer the *Smedley,* and that is not all, please. The *Smedley* is inquiring for the French vessel the *Aquitane.* So sorry."

The wrinkles on Mr. Kingman's face deepened. He did not speak for a moment, and Bob had never been so conscious of every personality. He heard Mrs. Kingman draw a choking breath that was almost like a sob.

"*Hein,*" he heard Oscar mutter, "*hein!*"

"Mac," he heard Mrs. Kingman say, and Mr. Kingman shook his head at her and Bob saw Mr. Kingman's fingers move toward the lock of his rifle.

"Please," Mrs. Kingman said, "*please,* Mac."

"Helen," Mr. Kingman's voice was still genial and pleasant, "you know me well enough not to say 'please.' You are quite right, Mr. Moto. You're a nice guy, Bob, but it's the — the game, isn't it? You today, Mr. Moto or me tomorrow. Helen, go down to the beach. We will call you in a few minutes. Who shall it be, Mr. Moto, you or me?"

Mr. Moto pulled out his purple handkerchief again. "Since it was your oversight, please," he said, "it would be so much nicer for you, Mr. Kingman, unless of course you are too friendly."

"Oh, well," said Mr. Kingman, "I was damned stupid. Go down to the beach, Helen. You wanted to pick up shells."

But Mrs. Kingman still waited. When she spoke again Bob had a feeling of gratitude which shook him, but it made him for the first time really believe in what was happening.

"But both of you were wrong," she said. "Only look at him. He isn't one of us."

"Oh," Mr. Kingman asked, "what makes you say that, Helen?"

Even then, when all sorts of thoughts were running through his mind, Bob Bolles was impressed by a discordant quality in her voice, by a sort of bitterness which he had never heard in it before.

"How can one explain a matter like that?" she said, and even her accent was different. "One can tell if one has been in the profession. Why, one can pick out the others like us in a crowded street. I saw it in your face even before I met you. Why, anyone can read it on this Japanese."

"Madame has so very much intuition," Mr. Moto said.

"It's the everlasting lying," she went on as though

she had not heard, "the everlasting trying to laugh and to smile when you're afraid, the watching and the danger. I have talked to Mr. Bolles and he hasn't it in him, not the personality nor the capacity."

Then Bob Bolles spoke for the first time. He must have been afraid — he was certainly afraid — but he still could not get it through his mind that he was the person who was standing there.

"That's right about my personality. The experts say there's something wrong with it."

Mr. Kingman smiled sympathetically. He seemed politely, mildly interested.

"So very nice to talk so," Mr. Moto said. "It shows your personality is very nice."

"No," said Mrs. Kingman, "it isn't that. Can't you see he's too honest?"

"My dear," Mr. Kingman said, "this isn't like you, Helen, to give way to emotion. Or are you emotionally interested in Mr. Bolles?"

Her face became a dull red. "No," she answered, "of course not."

"Then you had better go down to the beach," Mr. Kingman said, "unless, of course, you want to stay."

"No," she said, "I don't want to stay," and she turned quickly, as though she did not want to look at any of them, particularly at Bob Bolles, and walked past the palm-leaf huts toward the beach. They stood there waiting until she was out of sight.

"Too much emotion," Mr. Kingman said. "She is very good, but it is the difficulty with women. You are to be congratulated, Bob. You seem to have got further with her than I have."

It was only when he saw her walking away from him that Bob Bolles felt his first wave of panic. He had a sudden choking desire to run, to take the chance and to plunge into the bushes, and perhaps they hoped he would. He always thought that he would have run for it, if Mr. Moto had not spoken.

"If you have any messages, please," Mr. Moto said, "we should be so very glad. So customary with all of us."

Mr. Moto's voice steadied him. He put his hands in his pockets so that no one could see that they were shaking and he cleared his throat. He had the most absurd desire that no matter what happened he wanted Mr. Kingman and Mr. Moto to think that he had done it well.

"There's just one thing," he began.

Mr. Kingman looked sympathetic and kindly.

"Yes," he said, "go ahead, Bob. We don't want to hurry you."

It might not work, but if he could make them understand that they needed him, he might get out of it. He tried to keep his mind on that single point, although it was very hard to do, because his thoughts seemed to dart in all directions.

"This is all rather new to me," he said. "I guess everyone's been doing a lot of thinking. But have you thought who's going to sail that boat? You and Oscar can't do it, Mr. Kingman. You'll need a navigator to get out of here."

Bob Bolles felt his heart beating in his throat. There was no way of telling from watching them whether the idea was new or not. Mr. Kingman glanced at Mr. Moto. Mr. Moto's eyes grew narrow.

"So fortunate that I know navigation," Mr. Moto said.

"Perhaps you do," said Mr. Kingman. "That changes it a little. Perhaps you won't be going with us, Mr. Moto."

Suddenly Mr. Moto began to laugh.

"It is funny," he said, and Mr. Moto laughed again. It was the perfunctory laughter of his race, which did not have much humor in it. It appeared to annoy Mr. Kingman.

"What in — in hell is funny?" Mr. Kingman asked.

"So amusing," Mr. Moto said, "how all life hangs on little threads, so very, very delicate. Let us put it this way, please," Mr. Moto raised one finger. "I did not kill you, Mr. Kingman, because you understand the airplane. You did not eliminate me, because there is as yet no chance. Besides if the Americans are coming we must all work together."

"If they were coming," Mr. Kingman said, "they would have been here before now. How about it, Bob?"

Bob Bolles shook his head. He had not the least idea where the *Smedley* was, but he could tell that things were looking better.

"I'm not telling, of course," he said, "even if I knew."

Mr. Moto raised another finger.

"So serious," he said, "so very serious."

"Oh," Mr. Kingman said, "damn — damnation! I'm trying to think!"

"Yes," Mr. Moto said, "it is time to think. I am so sorry that I do not need him."

"Wait a minute," Bob Bolles said.

"Yes," said Mr. Moto, "yes?" And Bob Bolles grinned at him.

"Do you know the Caribbean well enough to get away if you're chased? I know nearly every harbor, Mr. Moto, in these waters. I know where to hide."

Mr. Moto expelled his breath softly between his teeth.

"No," he said. "I had not thought of that — if the destroyer is on its way — "

Mr. Kingman moved impatiently.

"Moto," he said, "maybe you and I'd better talk for a few minutes in private."

"Oh, yes," Mr. Moto said, "yes, I think it would be very nice."

Mr. Kingman beckoned to Oscar.

"Take Mr. Bolles down to the beach with Mrs. Kingman, Oscar, and keep an eye on him." And then he smiled. "Good-by. I'll see you later, Bob."

"Please," Mr. Moto said, "just a moment, Mr. Bolles. If this man with you should try to leave you, perhaps to shoot at me, will you call me, please?"

"With pleasure," Bob Bolles said, and Mr. Kingman began to laugh.

"By — by jingo, Mr. Moto!" Mr. Kingman said. "You really do think of everything."

Once several years before Bob Bolles had been piloting a training plane when the motor inexplicably had gone dead. The ship had gone out of control and was falling fast when, equally inexplicably, the motor had picked up again and he had been able to level off; but those few moments never wholly left him. His half mechanical, half pathetic efforts at the controls — while the certainty had grown on him that it was all over — always came back to him. When he heard the roar of the motor again, there had been a sort of nauseous, giddy weakness which in its way had been worse than that sense that he was through; and now the same feeling was with him. When he walked across the clearing toward the beach, with Oscar a pace or two behind him, Bob Bolles thought for a moment that he might be physically ill. The trees and the little bay — everything was blurred. He felt a sharp prod in the small of his back. It was Oscar poking him with the muzzle of his rifle.

"Get on, you," Oscar said, and Bob Bolles realized that he had stopped walking without knowing it. His vision cleared and Mercator Island and the bay were back, lonely, warm and beautiful. He heard the faint breeze in the palms again and the humming of insects and the chattering of birds.

"All right," he said, "all right, Oscar," and he began to walk again, and the sea and the air, everything, had a new beauty. The *Thistlewood* was still anchored in the harbor. He had never thought until then of human life as a factor in an intellectual problem which could be eliminated as easily as you crossed out a mathematical symbol with a pencil. He had never associated before with individuals who considered life in just those terms.

"You today," Mr. Kingman had said, "and Mr. Moto or me tomorrow." They were spies, the secret agents he had read about, but he had never seen a spy before. He had never considered before that he had led an immature, protected life; and now life was like walking on a tightrope across a chasm. Mr. Kingman and Mr. Moto had been so trained to it that they could move as easily as gymnasts in a circus, but he had not been trained to it, and now he was out on a wire balanced somewhere over the gap of infinity. Halfway across the clearing he stopped again and faced Oscar.

"Say, Oscar," he said, "how about rowing out to the boat and getting a drink? I need a drink."

"We go out to no boat," Oscar said, "and we get no drink."

"Oh, all right," Bob said, "but don't be so gloomy, Oscar."

He would not have lasted for a single minute if he had not known how to sail the *Thistlewood*. If Tom took the *Thistlewood* away, there would be no reason for him at all.

CHAPTER XI

"GO ON," Oscar said. "Keep walking."

"All right," Bob said. "I was just thinking about something, Oscar."

He was thinking that Tom was within earshot, watching them from somewhere. He had only to shout for Tom and Tom would come. He only had to tell Tom to forget what he had told him to do, and there was no reason why he shouldn't, for none of this business was his funeral. Yet he knew he would do no such thing. He would have to go ahead and take what was coming to him.

Mrs. Kingman was sitting on a log with her back toward them, looking at the sea. She did not move when she heard their footsteps. She did not move until he spoke.

"Hello," Bob Bolles said. Then she jumped up very quickly. She made a queer sort of picture in her gaily colored slacks and shirt, because the colors only emphasized the deadly whiteness of her face.

"It's all right," Bob said. "They haven't got me yet."

"Why — " she began. "Why — "

"Because someone had to sail the *Thistlewood,*" Bob said. "Oscar's down here to watch me so I won't get away, and Mr. Moto's having me watch Oscar so he won't get away."

She reached out her hand to him and he took it and her fingers gripped his very tight.

"Oh," she said, "I've been so — so sick! I'd have done anything, but there wasn't anything to do." When he thought of Mr. Kingman's eyes, he knew that she was right.

"Why, you did everything you could," he said. "I guess I'm in a bad way, but I'm glad you're not married to him."

"You behaved so well," she said. "I knew you would. Of course I'm not married to a man like that — or to anyone else. Are you still glad?"

"Yes," Bob said, "I am."

"If I'd been armed — " she began. "Where are they now?"

"Talking," he told her.

"Oh," she said, and she dropped his hand and turned to Oscar.

"Go and sit over by the bank," she said. "It's all right, Oscar."

"Yes, ma'm," Oscar answered, and he walked to the

edge of the beach and sat down with his rifle across his knees.

"We can talk," she said. "His English is very bad. I don't know where Mac picked him up. He's faithful and that's about all."

She had been shaken when he first appeared but now she was entirely different. It was as though she had cut herself away from any sentiment. She was beautiful, tranquilly beautiful, but now she had a new intensity, some purpose which he was sure had nothing to do with him. She was looking toward the ruined pier, where he had left Mr. Moto and Mr. Kingman, and her lips were twisted into an enigmatic little smile.

"He'd better take care," she said. She was not speaking to him — she was speaking to herself. Bob Bolles put his thumbs in his belt. He had not yet lost that sudden sense of gratitude that he was still alive and his new appreciation of everything around him included her. Somehow her disregard of him made him more completely conscious of her than he had ever been before.

"Who are you?" he asked. His question appeared to interrupt her train of thought and first she looked almost impatient at his interruption. Then she looked straight at him, as though she wanted him to have the truth whether he liked it or not.

"That's rather stupid of you," she answered. "You must know who I am, of course, and it doesn't hurt for you to know now. I'm a French national agent, under a special government bureau in Vichy. Now you don't like me any more, do you? Well, it doesn't make much difference."

"I don't know whether I like you or not," Bob said. "I don't know whether I've ever known one."

She laughed as though he had said something amusing, but her voice was kinder.

"You know one now," she said. "I'm not a nice girl for you to play with, because, you see — " She stopped and her voice grew harder. "You might as well know I'm the same as the rest of them."

"How do you mean?" Bob asked her.

"I mean," she answered, "I'd kill you, just as surely as Mac would, if it would help. In case you don't, I think you ought to know."

"I don't mind that," Bob said. She shook her head.

"My dear," she said, "I just wanted you to understand it. It seems fairer. You said you loved your country. I love mine. My mother was American, but my father was French."

"And Mr. Kingman?" Bob asked her. "Is he French?" He thought that her expression changed when he mentioned Mr. Kingman's name.

"I don't know what he is. Partly English, partly

Austrian, I think. He's a free lance, but he's been employed for this by our bureau. He's working with us now. At least," she hesitated, "as far as I can tell."

Bob Bolles did not answer and she went right on, confidentially, as though she were glad to speak to someone.

"There's a part of this plane which belongs to us, you know. There isn't any reason not to tell you. We need everything we can get for bargaining purposes now. We had definite word where the plane was left three weeks ago. I was sent to New York to meet someone," she hesitated, "a great friend of mine, and then word came that Mr. Kingman was to go here with me instead." She stopped and dug her toe in the white sand. She was watching him, but her dark sun glasses concealed her eyes. "I was surprised. I did not like it very much, but it was orders. I didn't like it then and I don't like it now."

"You mean, you don't trust him?" Bob asked. "You're afraid he may take it for himself? Well, I don't blame you much."

"Yes," she said slowly, "that's just what I mean."

"That's why you wanted me to take you here alone?" Bob asked.

"Yes," she said. "And now I'm going to ask you something." She paused and her voice had become insistent.

"Go ahead," Bob told her.

"Will you help me? Quickly. They'll be coming back."

Her words were slow, but they were perfectly distinct. Oscar was watching them, but he was nearly out of earshot.

"I guess you're right not to trust him," Bob said slowly.

"I shall get it anyway," she said. "But it would be easier if you helped. Will you?"

Bob Bolles drew a deep breath.

"I guess you're quite a girl," he said, "if you want to tackle Kingman. I'd like to help you, but I can't."

"Why not?" she asked.

"It isn't anything personal," Bob said.

"Hurry!" she said sharply. "I hear them." But he did not hurry. He was making up his own mind as much as speaking to her.

"You've been fair to me and I'll be fair to you. I don't know what this thing is, but my people want it — America wants it — and I'm going to try to get it — that's all." It was not all. It seemed strange for his mind to go back to it. He was thinking of Captain Burke on the *Smedley* and of his fitness report.

"I thought you'd say that," she said.

"All right," he answered. "I'm glad you thought so."

"But you can't," she said. "You mustn't. You don't know — "

"You're right there," he answered. "There's a lot I don't know." But he was learning more and more. He had learned a lot in the last hour.

"Be quiet," she said. "Here they come."

Her whole attention was centered on the path near the pier and she seemed to have forgotten him entirely. Mr. Moto and Mr. Kingman were walking across the sand toward them, side by side, like old friends. Then he heard her speaking to him again.

"Don't do anything. Don't try. People like us are only alive because we think of everything. Don't try, my dear. There's no chance for you at all." Then she called to them and waved her hand and Bob Bolles could almost believe that it was a pleasant party and that everyone was having a lovely time. Mr. Kingman and Mr. Moto were both smiling.

"Well, well," Mr. Kingman said, "here we all are again and everything is — is jake. Mr. Moto and I have been having a most constructive talk." Mr. Kingman paused and looked beyond the *Thistlewood* to the reef where the waves were beating and farther on out to the blank horizon. "There is this problem, my dear," he went on, "of — of possible outside intervention. Under the circumstances Mr. Moto and I have agreed to pool our resources temporarily."

"Oh," Mrs. Kingman said.

"I hope you'll rely on our judgment, my dear," Mr. Kingman went on. "We have agreed to join in accomplishing the first part of our mission here."

Mr. Moto smiled, placed his hand before his mouth and drew in his breath.

"Yes," he said, "yes, please."

Mrs. Kingman pursed her lips.

"I don't like it, Mac," she said.

Mr. Kingman looked hurt.

"My dear," he began, "there is really no reason for this personal pique, but let us — let us skip it. Now, you, Bob, it's a little different for you. You're here with us only because you have to be. Do you understand?"

"Yes," Bob said slowly, "I understand," but Mr. Kingman still seemed anxious to be plain.

"I hate to hurt people when it's unnecessary," he said. "No trying to leave us. No — no monkey business, old man. You must count yourself as lucky."

"Yes," Bob Bolles said slowly, "I know I'm lucky, Mac."

Mr. Kingman gave him a friendly pat on the shoulder.

"Then we're all — all okey-dokey?" he said.

"Oh, yes," said Mr. Moto, "yes."

"And there's no reason why we can't be agreeable. Now, what we are going to do is this, my dear. The plane cannot have been carried far from this landing. Mr. Moto has not been able to look far. We have decided to try the house on the hill first. If it is not there we shall have a bite of lunch and then Mr. Moto and I can prowl about the grounds. It should all be in — in the bag in a very few hours. Don't you agree, my dear?"

Mrs. Kingman looked happy again.

"Why, yes," she said. "Let's not keep standing in the sun."

"No," said Mr. Kingman, "we must — must speed it up. Heigh-ho, off to work we go!"

The suitcases and the hamper and the packsack were where they had left them. Oscar shouldered the pack and Bob picked up the hamper.

"Lead the way, Bob," Mr. Kingman said. "Heigh-ho!"

Mr. Moto scuttled over to the candlewood tree.

"My own bag," he said. "Ha-ha, I so nearly forgot."

He disappeared behind the tree, but in a few seconds he was back, carrying a small cheap fiber suitcase and a raincoat.

"By Jove," said Mr. Kingman, "I forgot that it might rain." But there was not a cloud in the sky.

Bob Bolles lifted the hamper to his shoulder and began walking slowly along the overgrown road that wound through the trees and vine-choked thickets.

In a few steps the breeze from the sea was gone and it was stiflingly hot. In a few more his shirt was soaked with perspiration.

"Heigh-ho," he heard Mr. Kingman humming just behind him, "heigh-ho!"

"Such lovely trees," he heard Mr. Moto saying. "Have you served before in the tropics, Mrs. Kingman?" Then the tone of his voice changed. "Ah, what's that?"

"Where?" Mr. Kingman asked sharply.

"No matter, please," said Mr. Moto. "Nothing."

But Bob Bolles had seen and it was not Mr. Kingman's fault that he had not, for no one could look everywhere at once. The road was still a grassy opening, stretching before them through the woods, and just as they had rounded a corner Bob Bolles had seen a copper-colored face staring at him from the thicket not twenty yards ahead. It was Tom, with his long nose and his ugly face. For just an instant Tom looked at him, frightened and inquiring, but even before Mr. Moto had spoken Bob had had time to shake his head and to jerk his thumb in the direction of the sea, and then Tom's face was gone. Bob Bolles felt his heart beat sickeningly in his throat.

"You look hot, Bob," he heard Mr. Kingman say.

"Yes," Bob answered. "I'm out of condition, I guess." His heart was beating very fast and the sweat was streaming down his face so that he had to blink his eyes. Tom was a good boy and he would do what he was told. The beach was clear and Tom would be down there in a little while. He would be in the dinghy, rowing to the *Thistlewood*. He would be out in the bow, slipping the anchor. Bob Bolles could hear his heart pounding.

"Bob," said Mr. Kingman.

"Yes, Mac," Bob said.

"I wonder what happened to that black boy of yours."

Bob Bolles cleared his throat.

"That boy was scared to death. He's hiding somewhere, Mac, and I wish — "

"Yes?" Mr. Kingman said.

"And I wish to God that I were with him," Bob Bolles said.

Mr. Kingman laughed and his voice was friendly.

"Now, Bob," he said, "we all get in — in a tight box sometimes."

Bob would have liked it better if Mr. Kingman had only been more typical and had answered more accurately one's preconceived ideas of what such a man should have been like. It was true what she had said. You could not guess his nationality. His thoughts, his motives, all were hidden beneath a sort of international veneer.

The old road had turned to the left and was winding steeply up the hill. You could see that it had been carefully built once, well surfaced with coral and shell, so that the heavy growth of trees and vines on either side had not yet grown across it. The road was open, and yet you could tell that it had not been used for years. Now and then a trail crossed it, made perhaps by wild pig, but there was no sign of a footpath. Clearly the Negroes on the island did not use the road. He began to make out a border of trees along its edges and he saw that the giant candlewoods which rose above the undergrowth must have been planted to shade the avenue when it was a clean white ribbon winding up the hill.

"By Jove, this is hot work," Mr. Kingman said. "Let's stop a moment for a — a breather, what?"

There it was again. He was speaking English when he thought he was speaking American. Bob Bolles halted and set the hamper down. The little party which was walking behind him single-file looked very hot, all except Mr. Moto.

"You mean 'take the weight off our feet' for a minute?" Bob Bolles said.

Mr. Kingman mopped his face with a fresh white handkerchief and laughed.

"Just what I meant to say, exactly!" he answered.

"Please, ah," Mr. Moto said, " 'take the weight off your feet,' does that mean to sit down, please?"

"Of course he means to sit down," Mrs. Kingman said, "and I think it's a very good idea."

"Please, ah," Mr. Moto said, "in the hot countries out of doors, so very careful where you sit down."

"Why?" Mrs. Kingman asked him. "You mean there are nettles?"

Mr. Moto drew his breath in delicately.

"Not vegetation always, please," he said. "In hot countries you sit and rest and many little bugs get in your, ah, garments."

It was hard to take Mr. Moto seriously, or Mr. Kingman either, there on the side of the hill. Mr. Kingman mopped his face again and looked thoughtfully up the glade of the old avenue.

"Are those gateposts there?" he asked.

Mr. Kingman's eyes were very good. He had picked out two masonry pillars, perhaps fifty yards ahead of them, which were so thickly covered with ferns and vines that they were hard to notice. The pillars were the entrance to the main grounds.

"You see," Bob Bolles said, "this was one of the old English plantations. They were usually laid out in the English tradition, with gates at the entrance of the main avenue. The quarters would be somewhere near here and the stables and the toolhouses.

There must have been cane fields on either side of us."

"Well," Mr. Kingman said, "let us go." And Bob Bolles picked up the hamper again.

The fields had been choked and covered long ago, but the double row of candlewoods still marked the old avenue and made the empty grassy road silent and shady. You could see, once you passed the gate, heaps of rubble and the walls of outbuildings.

"It may take a bit of looking," Bob heard Mr. Kingman say. "They might have stored it anywhere here. Look at that yonder. It is like a factory."

Mr. Kingman pointed through the trees to the right. The bare walls of a large rectangular building were rising up above the brush; and where part of a wall was breached and falling, you could distinguish a tangle of rusty metal.

"That would be the old mill," Bob Bolles said.

Mr. Kingman hesitated.

"Yes, it will take a bit of looking. That factory might be the place for it. I should not want to bring the thing any farther than I could help, would you, Moto? Shall we try in there?"

CHAPTER XII

MR. MOTO stared at the ruins through the trees. There was something very lonely about the sight of those walls still rising above the choking vegetation, seemingly struggling silently against the vines and ferns and bushes that were trying to pull them down. There was an echo of old violence about them, a memory of destruction and burning and pillage. Bob Bolles heard Oscar clear his throat.

"Them niggers," Oscar said, "they burned it, what?"

It was more than Oscar had said for a long while. In some way the place must have impressed him and must have somehow shocked some innate sense of thrift and order. "Them dirty niggers!" Oscar said. "By damn, yes it all was burnt!"

It must have all happened a century before, but there was still a strong impression of old destruction, the same sense of lost endeavor which Bob Bolles had once felt when he had visited the ruins of a great French estate in Haiti. On either side of the road were the crumbling remains of large and small buildings.

"I like it the way it is," Mr. Kingman said. "It is sad. It looks almost like a town."

Mr. Moto coughed and looked up at the sky and then at his wrist-watch.

"It was all so long ago," he said. "May I make a suggestion, please? If we go to the house first, there will be a view of the sea. I should like so very much to be sure there is nothing coming. Someone, I think, should watch."

Mr. Kingman looked troubled and he nodded.

"You're right, Moto," he said. "We had better take a look. We'll go on to the house."

They began climbing slowly up the hill again and no one spoke for a while. Bob Bolles could feel the urgency of their thoughts and he was thinking, too. His whole life kept moving through his thoughts.

"Come on, Bob," he heard Mr. Kingman say behind him. "Step — step on it!"

"All right, Mac," he answered.

His breath was coming fast from the climb, but his voice was perfectly steady. It was his great desire to be steady, although it could make no possible difference. His main hope was that he would behave well. They might not care, but he wanted Kingman and Moto to know that he could take it as well as they could and he wanted Mrs. Kingman to know it.

"Ah!" he heard Mr. Kingman say behind him. "Well, there it is."

They had rounded a curve in the avenue and the ruins of Westerly Hall lay in front of them. Bob never forgot his first view of the house. Somehow its grim solidity conveyed the impression of what it must have been once, and somehow its past was stronger than its present. It must have been a fine house once, a square three-story mansion, overlaid with stucco. Now its roof was down and the stucco was peeling in a sickly way, revealing huge patches of the gray coral stone beneath it. The kitchen quarters were a mass of weeds. The tall arched windows and the great front door were black and gaping, but all the ground around the house was clear, perhaps because the knoll where it stood was exposed to the prevailing breeze. Thus there was an impression, even then, of lawns and terraces. It was still possible to trace the curve of the avenue, which ended at massive steps that led to a broad stone terrace on which the house stood — a terrace with battered stone railings that overlooked the sea. On a medallion above the door, you could still see the coat of arms of the family and, in spite of the watchful bleakness, there was a sense of vanished hospitality, of servants and mahogany. The house was there in an utterly forgotten world of its own. Bob would not have been surprised if he had seen the front door open, although no door was there. Instead, a flock of gray birds flew chattering from one of the lower windows and the breeze was on his face again, clear and fresh from the sea.

"Oh," he heard Mrs. Kingman say, "it must have been beautiful once."

"Yes," Mr. Kingman said, "but never mind it now."

He was opening the case that contained his field glasses. To the left, as they stood facing the great front door, down below them, was a wide blue stretch of ocean. The waves near the horizon glinted in the sunlight and, nearer to the land, the breakers churned in a white ring around the coral reef.

"Well," Mr. Kingman said, "it all looks clear."

"Yes," Mr. Moto answered. "I am so glad to think so. Let us walk up the steps. Up there is a better view."

Bob climbed up quickly. He wanted to see the bay which was still concealed by the top of trees, but up on the terrace the pier and the beach were all distinct beyond the tree-tops, not half a mile away. Mr. Kingman was looking through his glasses again.

"What — " he said. "What the devil? The boat is moving!"

You did not need glasses to see it. Bob Bolles felt a strange sense of elation, and a grim and inexplicable desire to laugh. The *Thistlewood* in the distance, like a child's toy boat, was nosing her way through the reef to the open sea. He could see Tom, a small black dot, standing at the wheel. Bob Bolles set down the hamper and turned and faced them. Oscar had dropped his suitcase.

"Why," Mrs. Kingman said, "the anchor rope must have broken!"

Mr. Moto's face was impassive, but his voice was high and reedy.

"No," he said, "it is under power. Someone is aboard, I think." And he glanced sideways at Bob Bolles.

"It looks that way, doesn't it?" Bob said.

Mr. Kingman snapped his glasses back into their case. In almost the same instant he had unslung his rifle from his shoulder and for just a second he looked at Bob Bolles thoughtfully.

"So that's it, is it?" he said.

"Yes," Bob Bolles said evenly, "I told him to take her off if he had a chance."

If it was the last speech that he had made on earth, he was glad that he had been able to make it. He had taken a good deal from them that day. He smiled at Mrs. Kingman. He had thought that they would be angry, but the strange thing was, no one was angry. Mr. Moto stood rubbing the back of his head and gazing at the harbor. Mr. Kingman was adjusting the sights on his rifle.

"Give me the telescope sight," he said, "and some

extra clips, please, Oscar. It cannot be more than six hundred yards."

"It will do no good," said Mr. Moto. "You kill him and the boat goes on the rocks."

"We'll get her off," said Mr. Kingman briskly. "The telescope sight and the clips, please, Oscar. Damn it, hurry up! What's the matter?"

Oscar had not moved and his face was red.

"I have left the sight," he said, "and I only took four clips of shells. I have thought we go back aboard."

"Hell," Mr. Kingman said, "hell's fire!" He knelt down and rested his rifle on the stone railing. *Smack!* the rifle went. *Smack! Smack! Smack!* And Mr. Kingman laughed pleasantly.

"Ah, he's running from the wheel!"

Smack! the rifle went. Mr. Kingman, smiling faintly, reached in his pocket for another clip.

"Don't you think," Bob Bolles asked, "that you're wasting your time?"

"Why?" Mr. Kingman asked, looking up at him from the rifle sights.

"Because he's lashed the wheel and gone below," Bob said. "You can shoot her full of holes, but you won't stop her, Mac."

Mr. Moto still rubbed the back of his head. He was smiling, but his smile was mechanical.

"So little use to tell Mr. Kingman that," Mr. Moto

said. "It might have been better for you later if he had used more shots."

Mr. Kingman thrust home the fresh clip and got up from his knees. The lines of his face were deeper and he did not speak for a moment.

"I've got plenty left," he said. "Well, that was quite a play, Bob." He took off his sun helmet and rubbed the back of his hand across his forehead. "There's no use being angry. I don't like to get angry, but this is a — a hell of a mess."

Mrs. Kingman spoke sharply.

"It's your own fault," she began. "Mac, why didn't you think?"

"Please be quiet," said Mr. Kingman. "I cannot think of everything." And he drummed his fingers thoughtfully on the stock of his rifle.

They must have all been staring at the harbor, lining the edge of the terrace, their backs to the house. Bob Bolles never dreamed, and he did not believe anyone else did either, that they were not entirely alone up there, looking at the sea — until he heard a voice behind him. There was no warning — only a full, throaty voice.

" 'Ere, 'ere," the voice said. "What's all this how-do-you-do? The vessel has gone, hasn't it?"

When Bob Bolles thought of it afterwards, he supposed that the instant which followed would have been amusing, if anyone had possessed the capacity to appreciate it. It always seemed to him so incongruous that in some ways it was magnificent. Almost in unison, they all stared over their shoulders, like children caught in some guilty act.

"My God," said Mr. Kingman, and there was no doubt that his nerves were very good, for he was the first to recover, "where did you drop from, my man?"

It seemed to Bob Bolles the only possible question to ask. Standing on the terrace just behind them was Inspector Jameson of the Kingston police.

The Inspector's clothing was somewhat dingy and soiled, but even so it had the uncompromising military neatness that Bob Bolles remembered in Kingston a few days back. The Inspector's military mustache was carefully trimmed. His puffy red cheeks were clean-shaven. Like Mr. Kingman, he was wearing a sun helmet and in his right hand he held a short stick, a swagger stick. It made him look like what he undoubtedly had been once — an English noncommissioned officer.

"It will hardly help to bluster," Inspector Jameson said, "and I shall give everyone here the usual warning. Anything said by him, or her," — his stolid blue eyes moved in the direction of Mrs. Kingman, — "will be used against him or her."

From the way Inspector Jameson spoke, he seemed

to consider that his sudden appearance there was only a routine matter.

"And I might add," Inspector Jameson said, "it will do no good to flourish those weapons at me."

"Oh," said Mr. Kingman, "won't it?"

"You'll only be responsible for the death of an officer in line of duty," Inspector Jameson said, "besides what else is against you. It will 'ardly help you, sir."

Mr. Kingman had a dazed, blank look — and they must have all looked the same. From the corner of his eye Bob Bolles saw that Oscar was watching Mr. Kingman's face. Mr. Kingman moved his hand and Oscar moved a little to the left. Inspector Jameson must have seen the gesture.

"It's too late for monkey tricks for you or that Swede either," Inspector Jameson said.

But Mr. Kingman's voice had only surprise in it.

"Never mind that now," Mr. Kingman said. "Can't you tell us where the devil you came from?"

The Inspector's official manner relaxed slightly.

"No harm in explaining," he answered more genially. "In the motor launch with this Japanese gentleman, of course," and he pointed a heavy finger at Mr. Moto.

"Excuse," Mr. Moto said. "There were two in the crew. I did not see you."

"No more you did," Inspector Jameson answered,

185

"since I was stowed snug up forward. Why, you can thank me that you had the launch at all." The Inspector was only human. He looked at Mr. Moto complacently.

"Oh," said Mr. Moto. "Please, why should you want — "

"It isn't always foreigners who know everything, if I may say so," Inspector Jameson answered. "How did you think it was so easy for a foreigner like you to hire a boat? Why, I'll tell you why — because the police have been searching for a Swede under the name of Oscar Lindquist and for a gentleman with an American passport by the name of Kingman."

Mr. Kingman's face was as motionless as marble, but he did not speak.

"But I am not Mr. Kingman, please," Mr. Moto said.

"No more you're not and very lucky for you," Inspector Jameson answered. "You shall explain later why you were looking for Mr. Kingman. When it was known you were asking where he was and looking for a boat, it was a welcome opportunity, if I do say so. I arranged for the boat and I 'opped aboard and when she passed the schooner I knew that I was right and when she got here I 'opped off and now — "

"I do not understand," Mr. Kingman said.

Inspector Jameson squared his shoulders and gave his stick an expert twirl.

"Now that the schooner is gone, the jig is up, Mr. Kingman, for you and for the Swede here named Oscar Lindquist. You are 'ere on an island, one of His Majesty's possessions, and no way of getting off, and I'm 'ere representing the law, sir, and that's all there is to it."

A blank, incredulous look crossed Mr. Kingman's face.

"But I don't exactly see — " Mr. Kingman said. "Where is your boat now, man?"

Inspector Jameson spoke respectfully. He obviously considered that Mr. Kingman was a step above all the others.

"Once the schooner was sighted last night," he said, "I knew you were aboard and coming to Mercator. The motorboat has orders to go on and send for a Government cutter. I wanted no accident about it, in case you should get to the schooner again, and there are odd doings here which need investigation. But now the schooner's gone you can't get off and I've showed myself. That's all, sir."

Mr. Kingman pursed his lips. He seemed to whistle noiselessly.

"And I take it," the Inspector went on, "from what I overheard 'ere, the black boy employed by Mr. Bolles has run off with the schooner for what reason I cannot fancy. And what brings this lady and all the rest of you here is something for further investigation when the authorities appear on the cutter. In the meanwhile, since no one can leave here, I'm taking over. Is that plain to everyone?"

"Yes," said Mr. Moto. "Thank you. The cutter — when is it coming back, please?"

Inspector Jameson looked up at the sun and then glanced at his wrist-watch. He was magnificent in his complete faith in himself. He seemed entirely oblivious of any possible danger.

"If she is at Nevis she should be here by noon tomorrow," he said. "It's as I say, the jig is up, Mr. Kingman. You can't get off and you won't be so foolish as to lay a hand on me. Your 'istory's been sent on the cable from Scotland Yard, — a sort of international toff, I take it you are, — and you won't make matters worse for you by lying an 'and on me, if nothing can be gained by it. You nor anyone else."

His china-blue eyes moved serenely across the group and Mr. Kingman stood with his mouth half open.

"Do you mean to say that you're here by yourself, my good man?" Mr. Kingman asked. "You mean you haven't got anyone lurking in the bushes?"

"Here by myself is right, sir," the Inspector answered. "One man is enough when he has the old Empire behind him."

Mr. Kingman looked at Mr. Moto in a stupefied sort of way.

"Did you ever hear of anything like this?" he asked.

"Yes," Mr. Moto said, "please, it is like the British."

"By — by Jove," Mr. Kingman said, "I never can understand them," and then Bob Bolles spoke up. He could not endure standing there and doing nothing.

"Jameson," he began, "you damned fool — "

" 'Ere," said Inspector Jameson. "That's no way to talk, Mr. Bolles. I do not believe you are in any ways implicated, but there must be an explanation."

"Wait, please," Mr. Moto said. "Why do you want Mr. Kingman and the other man, please?"

Inspector Jameson straightened his shoulders again.

"Quite right for you to ask," the Inspector said, "I'm sure," and his voice became official and sonorous. "On a very serious charge. On the confession of a keeper of a public house — one Henry Pasquez."

"Oh," said Mr. Kingman, "that's it, is it?"

"There you have it, sir," said Inspector Jameson, nodding. "On the night of November 12th, Henry Pasquez was apprehended endeavoring to conceal a body."

There was a sharp cry from Mrs. Kingman, but the Inspector's voice went on.

"The body of a tourist, French, described as Charles Durant. The confession describes one Oscar Lindquist as strangling this Charles Durant with a rope in a very 'orrible way, if I may say so."

"Oh," Mrs. Kingman cried, "you — "

Mr. Kingman turned on her. His face was white, but his eyes were burning bright.

"You be quiet if you know what's good for you," he said. "What other piece of nonsense is there, Mr. Policeman?"

"And you are accused as accessory," Inspector Jameson said. "I 'ereby place you under arrest and anything you say will be used — "

Mr. Kingman's voice rose in a sharp snarl.

"Against me? What? All right, Oscar!"

And Mr. Kingman drove the butt of his rifle with all his force into the pit of Inspector Jameson's stomach. At the same moment Bob Bolles felt a hand on his arm.

"Not now, please," Mr. Moto said, "careful, Mr. Bolles!"

It was over in a second. Inspector Jameson and Oscar were struggling on the stone terrace. Mr. Kingman was leaning over them, but almost instantly he looked up.

"Be careful, my dear," he said to Mrs. Kingman. "Keep back!" His voice was sharp and harsh above the other sounds. Oscar had raised his fist and had struck with all his force at the base of the Inspector's skull, and now the Inspector lay still.

"All right," said Mr. Kingman briskly. "No need to

finish him, Oscar. Drag that fool into the shade and put a gag in his mouth and tie him up."

Oscar was very strong. He lifted the whole limp weight of the Inspector on his shoulders and carried him around a corner of the house and out of sight. Mr. Kingman looked at Mr. Moto as though he expected his sympathy and understanding.

"He'll be all right for the time being, I think," Mr. Kingman said. "By — by Jove, I never saw a thing like that. He was going to arrest all of us. He really meant it."

But Mr. Moto did not appear to sympathize and he shook his head slowly.

"So very bad, please," he said. "This brings more trouble, always more trouble. Why liquidate a man in Kingston, Mr. Kingman?"

Mr. Kingman moved his head impatiently. He seemed to be troubled too. He seemed to be using all his will to keep his nerves under proper control.

"Damn it," Mr. Kingman said, and he spoke jerkily. "That man — that Henry — was recommended to me. I told the fool to make it look like suicide. By God, I even fixed the farewell note. How did I know he'd lose his nerve? At any rate, it was necessary."

Mr. Moto moved his left hand softly over the creases of his white coat.

"I should never do such a thing in Kingston," he said softly. "There are other ways."

"Damn it," Mr. Kingman said, again. "It's none of your business, and there was a difference of opinion and the man fought. And that's that. It was an accident, and you can't help accidents."

Then Mrs. Kingman spoke — so unexpectedly that even Mr. Moto looked startled.

"You coward!" she said. Her eyes were icy cold and contemptuous and her lips were curved with the same contempt. "You double-dealing coward! You meant to go back on us all the time, didn't you?" Mr. Kingman took a quick step backwards. His eyes were on Mr. Moto, but Mr. Moto did not move. Suddenly Mr. Kingman's face looked as ugly as a snake's.

"Perhaps I'd better explain myself," Mr. Kingman said, "right now."

"Yes," said Mr. Moto, "it would be so nice."

"Then, listen," Mr. Kingman said. "It's better to have it in the open. I'm out for myself entirely. To hell with the Vichy Government and any sniveling Frenchmen! Helen, my dear, you people don't pay enough. It was an accident in Kingston and I'm sorry for it. Mr. Moto and I are working together now, and perhaps we'll continue if Mr. Moto pays enough. That part on the plane should be worth a million dollars if it's delivered to the right party. But as for you,

Helen, you're out of it. You've always been out of it. You and your people can't stop me now." Mr. Kingman paused and moistened his lips. No one spoke until he went on again.

"All this happily married business! I'm just as sick of it as you are. If you know what's good for you — and I think you do — you'll play this game with me right to the end. And no further personal remarks from you, my dear. There's nothing you can do — absolutely nothing. You're in a damned tough spot and you know it. Do I make myself clear?"

There was something sickeningly certain about Mr. Kingman's speech. It was full of all sorts of unspoken implications, and Mrs. Kingman must have understood it. She was standing stiffly, digging her nails into her palms. Her lower lip was trembling and for a moment Bob Bolles thought she was going to weep.

"Yes," she said, "it's clear."

"And you'll do what I tell you, won't you?" Mr. Kingman said.

"Yes," she answered, "yes, Mac," and she seemed utterly beaten, utterly resigned.

"You've got a great way with women, haven't you?" Bob Bolles asked. "I'd like to take that up with you someday." He had to say something. He could not have stopped if he had tried, for he suddenly felt himself seething with white-hot anger. It was not what Mr. Kingman said, but what he had not said. And then Oscar came around the corner of the house, holding his rifle ready.

"It is all right, Oscar," Mr. Kingman said, and his eyes met Bob Bolles's squarely. "Romantic, aren't you, Bob? She's pretty. I'll admit it. And if I wanted she'd get down on her face right now and lick the dust off my shoes, because she'd have to, Bob, if she knows what's good for her. Don't interrupt. I'm taking up your case. That was pretty smart of you, sending that boat away, wasn't it? There's just one thing about it — "

"What?" Bob asked.

"It makes you about as useless as a broken-down horse, my friend, unless you can think of some way of getting that boat back."

"To hell with you," Bob Bolles said. "There isn't any way. She's gone. They'll pick you up in the morning, Kingman."

"That's just a little hasty," Mr. Kingman said, "don't you think? I'm going to give you time to think that one over. When the breath is being shut out of you, you may change your mind — 'a 'orrible death with a rope.' You heard that, didn't you? Oscar can handle that."

Bob Bolles still felt that white flame of anger, but his mind was working fast.

"Maybe Mr. Moto wouldn't like it," he said.

Mr. Kingman's forehead wrinkled.

"I do not see — " Mr. Moto said. "Why should I not like it?"

Bob Bolles answered quickly. He still had a card to play.

"It just occurred to me," he said. "You wanted a plane mechanic. I know a lot about airplane engines, Moto. I can put them together and take them down. I was an aviator, in case it interests you."

"By — by Jove," Mr. Kingman said, "I didn't know that."

"I just thought Mr. Moto would like to know," Bob Bolles answered.

"Why, yes," said Mr. Moto. "Thank you so much. That is very interesting."

Mr. Kingman's fingers drummed gently on his rifle stock.

"You think damned fast, don't you?" he asked. "Well, Moto and I might be able to use you, Bob. And now, Mr. Moto — "

"Yes," Mr. Moto said, "yes, please?"

"You're pretty much in the way too, but we need each other, don't we, in case the American Navy or that British cutter comes? We're two against you, Moto, and we're agreed to do nothing until we find that plane. That's right, isn't it?"

"Yes," said Mr. Moto, "that is right."

"And maybe we can talk business afterwards."

"Yes," said Mr. Moto, "yes, perhaps."

"Then take your hand out of your pocket," Mr. Kingman said. "It's all right, Moto."

Mr. Moto did not remove his hand from his coat pocket.

"Excuse me, please," he said, "if under the circumstances I still do not trust you altogether."

Mr. Kingman shrugged his shoulders. That genial manner of his was back with him again.

"Oh," he said, "all right, all right. Let's have a bite of lunch and then we'll start looking," and he glanced toward the house. "Bring in the basket, Oscar. There should be some place to sit inside."

"Why, yes," said Mrs. Kingman. "I'm very hungry now."

It was all surprising to Bob Bolles. That anger of hers and her fear seemed to have entirely gone, just as though that scene with Mr. Kingman had never happened. It was most amazing — that complete control of hers. She seemed completely happy again. Perhaps she was always meant to be happy.

CHAPTER XIII

THEY HAD all turned by then toward the stone walls of the house with their peeling yellow stucco. The tall windows of the room in front of them opened like doors upon the terrace and showed a large bare room inside with a flagstone floor. Fire and weather had destroyed the beams and ceilings long ago, so that the room itself was half choked with rubble and you could look up through the three stories of the house to the open sky; but a corner of the room near the windows was clear and, standing in the corner, you were in the shell of the greater house with all its ground plan bare and bleak in spite of the wreckage. The room where they stood might have been the dining room or the parlor, and it had the only floor which was left. Beyond it was the entrance hall with the remains of a stone staircase which led upwards into emptiness. The floor of the hallway and the floors of the other rooms had dropped into the cellars and the floor of the room where they were standing would have been gone long ago had there been a cellar beneath it. As it was, there were the remains of plaster on the wall and a fireplace between two windows that was half filled with rubbish.

"Why," Mrs. Kingman said, "there isn't anything here," and Mr. Kingman and Mr. Moto also seemed surprised for, with its walls still standing, the building from the outside still gave the appearance of a house.

"The devil," Mr. Kingman said, "there's no place here to store a plane. By Jove, there's law and order! There's the British Empire."

He was referring to Inspector Jameson, who was standing, trussed and gagged, against a heap of stones. There was nothing to do about Inspector Jameson then.

Oscar said nothing. He pulled four blocks of stone together to make a table and moved some other stones around it for seats. Then he found some tin cups that were in the picnic hamper and pulled out a bottle of wine.

"Isn't Oscar wonderful?" Mrs. Kingman said. "He can make any place look like home." Bob Bolles sighed. He could not make her out at all.

"Yes," said Mr. Kingman. Nothing seemed to disturb him, not even Inspector Jameson. Those people had amazing resilience. There was no doubt of that. "Now, we all feel better for the moment, don't we?

The walls protect us from the sun, and here is canned chicken and bread, and Oscar will boil some coffee, I think. Pass the cups around, Helen, my dear. It is Rüdesheimer, if no one objects to a German wine. Sit down, Moto. Sit down, Bob. Your troubles haven't started yet, my boy."

And Mr. Kingman sat down, resting his rifle across his knees. He raised his cup, but Bob noticed that his other hand still held the rifle.

"Very pleasant wine," Mr. Moto said. "I have always admired all things German."

"Germany used to be a very restful place," Mr. Kingman said. "Here's looking at you, Mr. Policeman. I'm sorry you can't have a drink of it too," and Mr. Kingman laughed. "Odd, isn't it, all of us sitting here at cross-purposes — Mr. Moto with his hand in his pocket, me watching him, and Bob there, wishing he could break my neck? By — by Jove, it's rather jolly, isn't it? Here comes the coffee. Have some, Moto?"

"Yes," said Mr. Moto and he made a gentle belching sound. "Thank you very much."

"Yes," said Mr. Kingman, "all together and all at cross-purposes, all ready to fly apart at a moment's notice. It will be quite a while before I can come back here again, I think. Yes, this is the — the life, isn't it? Helen, my dear, I'm glad you're taking it so well."

She looked at him across the stones.

"It's the only way there is to take it, Mac," she said.

"After all, that man Durant was just another of us. He was nothing serious to you, was he, my dear?"

"Just another of us," Mrs. Kingman said. "That's all."

"By Jove," Mr. Kingman went on, "here's our little snack of luncheon over and I doing all the talking — the — the life of the party, what? There's just one thing we've got to think about — some way of getting off this island — and, Bob, you're going to do the thinking for us." Mr. Kingman got to his feet. "Helen, my dear, if I may talk to you outside for a minute, we must think of some way for Bob to get that schooner of his back here. Will you excuse us, please?"

Mr. and Mrs. Kingman walked out on the terrace, and Mr. Moto and Bob Bolles were alone except for Oscar, who sat some distance away watching them. Mr. Moto glanced toward Inspector Jameson and then took a noisy sip of his coffee. His face was devoid of any expression. The events of the morning did not appear to have disturbed him in the least.

"If you have some signal to call back your boat I think it would be so much nicer if you told," Mr. Moto said; "so much nicer — because Mr. Kingman will make you tell. There are so many ways."

"To hell with all that," Bob Bolles said. "I can take anything that you boys dish out."

Mr. Moto laughed politely.

"You are very nice, Mr. Bolles," he said, "very, very nice. I only suggested, please — soon it will be difficult for all of us."

Bob Bolles looked at him curiously.

"That thing on the plane — " Bob Bolles asked him suddenly. "What's your game? Are you going to get it for yourself, or are you going to play in with Kingman? Not that it's any of my business, I suppose."

Mr. Moto set down his cup.

"So very pleased you asked," he said. "I think in the end I shall have it for myself, yes, when the time comes."

"Suppose Kingman's a Nazi?" Bob asked. "You're playing in with those boys, aren't you?"

Mr. Moto looked interested.

"Oh," he said, "do you think he is a Nazi? Why, please?"

"Well, you take Oscar," Bob said. "First he pretended he was a Swede and now he's developed a German accent. And take Mr. Kingman's accent."

Mr. Moto's gold teeth glittered in a friendly smile.

"So clever of you, I think," he said. "Mr. Kingman has suggested the same himself. I am so sorry I do not trust him — a very bad man, I do not like Mr. Kingman."

"I don't blame you," Bob Bolles said fervently. "I hate his guts."

"So happy to hear your thoughts," Mr. Moto said. "But I beg you, please, Mr. Bolles, to take care of yourself. I am so glad you understand airplanes, Mr. Bolles. But take care of yourself." Mr. Moto's narrow, dark eyes darted a glance in the direction of the terrace. "So sorry there should be trouble between America and Japan — two such very nice nations. It is all a cultural misunderstanding."

Bob tried to make his voice sound careless. Mr. Moto was leading up to something, he was very sure. The slender bonds of expediency which were holding them together were shifting and wearing very thin.

"You and I," Bob said, "might reach a temporary cultural understanding."

Mr. Moto sucked in his breath noisily between his teeth.

"Please," he said, "no understanding now."

Bob had nearly forgotten Oscar. Oscar had risen from the stone where he had been sitting close to Inspector Jameson. Now he stepped across the space to the stone table, scowling.

"By damn," Oscar said, "you shut your mouth or I shut it for you."

"Please," Mr. Moto began, "I think — "

He stopped. Mr. Kingman had walked in from the terrace with Mrs. Kingman just behind him.

"Here," Mr. Kingman asked. "What's the trouble here?"

Oscar was still scowling.

"By damn," Oscar said, and he stabbed the muzzle of his rifle at Bob Bolles. "He talked to the Yap."

Mr. Kingman laughed.

"All right, Oscar, let him talk," Mr. Kingman said. "Perhaps you can have your fun with him later. Bob, I'm leaving Helen here to reason with you. She's a very sensible girl and a nice girl, isn't she? We've got to find some way of getting that boat back. I'd like a painless way. She wants to try to help you, Bob, don't you, my dear? And, Moto, you and I'd better start looking for that plane. We'll go down and try that sugar factory. Are you ready?"

Mr. Moto bowed.

"It has been so pleasant. We have stayed so long," he said. "Yes, all ready."

"Well," Mr. Kingman said, "then everything is hunky — hunky-dory, isn't it? Oscar, keep an eye on Mr. Bolles. If he makes a jump for it, you know what to do. And if you get a chance give that policeman a little water. We may need him later. You never can tell. Come on, Moto."

Mr. Kingman and Mr. Moto walked out on the terrace.

"Heigh-ho," Mr. Kingman was humming, "heigh-ho!"

Bob Bolles stood listening to their footsteps and then he said: —

"It's nice to be rid of him for a while. I wish I had a gun."

Mrs. Kingman was holding her sun glasses delicately between her thumb and forefinger.

"Don't talk that way," she said. "You see, he knows I care about you. He's awfully, awfully clever."

"Care about me?" Bob Bolles repeated. He was utterly surprised. It was all so strange, given the time and place.

"Let's go out on the terrace," Mrs. Kingman said. "I don't like it here, and be careful. Oscar's watching."

They walked across the terrace and sat on the stone railing, while Oscar sat in the shadow of the gaping window, holding his rifle. Bob could see Mr. Moto and Mr. Kingman, like two old friends, walking down the old avenue in the direction of the sugar factory — a logical place to look, since there had been nothing in the house — and he watched them disappear beneath the trees. When he looked at the blue of the sea and the waves on the reefs, when he saw the blackish green contours of the island and its red volcanic earth, he could almost believe that he had been asleep, that Inspector Jameson had never appeared, that there had been no talk of sudden death. But parts of it were still with him, and last of all, that amazing speech of hers. It came so suddenly that he could hardly believe it.

"Do you mean that?" he asked.

She was sitting on the rail beside him, looking not at him but straight ahead of her at nothing.

"Oh, God," she said, "of course I mean it! It happened somewhere on the boat, I suppose, or somewhere in Kingston. How do those things happen? I don't know. On the beach this morning — I don't know. But he knew. He can see through everything. There isn't even time to be nice about it. He'll use it if he can. And he says you care for me. Do you?"

He heard her question, but he did not answer immediately. Somehow he had never thought of it that way. He thought that he had been puzzled by her and sorry for her, but there had been something else. All at once he seemed to see it perfectly clearly.

"Why, yes, I do," he said, "now you mention it, but I don't know why."

"Nobody knows why," she said. "You were probably lonely, and I was sorry for you at first. Nobody knows why. But that's why he left us here."

"It's funny," Bob said. "I've never told you anything I've thought about you, and this doesn't seem to be the time or place, but listen — "

He was still surprised by it. He still found it hard to believe.

"Yes?" she asked. "What is it?"

"If I can get Oscar's rifle away from him — go up

and talk to him and let me get behind him — we can get out of this yet."

His instinct had always been for direct action. In his present mood nothing would have made him more completely happy than to get his hands on Oscar. If he could get near enough, he was strong enough to handle it. Perhaps because she was sitting beside him he felt a complete confidence in his strength. Once he was through with Oscar, he could untie Inspector Jameson. Jameson was stupid, but he was a good stout man. If he was not armed, and probably he was not, at least they would have Oscar's rifle between them.

"Come on. What do you say?" Bob asked. "Get me near enough so I can jump him and we'll bust this thing wide open."

From the way she looked he might have been telling her that she was beautiful, and she was almost unbelievably pretty — her slacks, her shirt with the little sailboats, her broad-brimmed straw hat. In spite of everything she still looked like a girl who was on a pleasant picnic. She seemed to be smiling at her own thoughts, staring straight ahead at nothing.

"No, dear," she said. "We might — but I'm not sure. I have to be sure. I'm going to play it another way. It's Mac I'm interested in. It's Mac — and that part on the plane." She looked down at her dark glasses. "You see, that's what I'm here for. I want that part of the plane."

"But you can't get it," Bob began. "When he gets back — "

"You're wrong there, dear," she answered quietly. "I think I can. At least I'm going to try. That's what I'm here for. Wait. We'll both wait and see."

He knew then what it was he had always seen in her. It was something which had nothing to do with him, something which he'd never be able to touch. She had warned him of it down there on the beach.

"Nothing's going to stop you, is it?" he asked. "I can see that. I guess I've always seen it."

"That's true, dear," she said. "Nothing's going to stop me."

"Well," he answered, "I guess that's why I love you. I said I didn't know, but that's why."

"It's sweet of you to say it," she answered, "because it's so impossible, and we can't think about ourselves now, not at all. And I'd give anything, almost any-thing — " And then her voice broke. "It's sad, it's awfully sad. Don't say you love me again."

"We'll get out of this," Bob said. "I'll tell you later."

"Don't," she said, "please don't. Of course you ought to tell me now. We ought to tell each other all about each other, because it's so beautiful here. I wish that time could stop. I wish we could be here always."

"With that low-lived gangster sitting in the win-dow with a gun?" Bob asked.

"No," she said. "But suppose we owned this island. Suppose we built a house here. Look at the color on the sea."

The harbor below them was sapphire blue and the water by the reefs was emerald and out by the horizon there were streaks of purple on it. Somehow it was important, although he could not tell why, and he never forgot that moment, sitting beside her and looking at the sea.

"But we can't talk about it now," she said. "Perhaps not ever, not any of it. You must listen to me, dear."

"Yes," he said, "I'm listening."

"You've never seen a man like Mac, but you know a little what he's like now, and he's going to be worse. He's got to get off this island or he'll be hanged. That was a mistake he made in Kingston. He's desperate, I think."

"All right," Bob said simply. "I hope to God he is. I'm pretty desperate myself."

"Listen, please," she said. "When you sent Tom away you must have arranged some signal to call him back. Mac knows it. Everybody knows it."

"Suppose he does," Bob asked. "Then what?"

"He's going to ask you and you've got to tell him."

"Oh, no, I won't," Bob said.

"You've got to, dear, or he'll make you. You don't

believe it, but you'll tell him in the end. I know. I've seen it. Please — No, wait. I'll tell you something else."

"What?" Bob asked.

The insistence in her voice changed into a note of grimness.

"It won't change what's going to happen. It won't do any good."

"What's going to happen?" Bob asked.

She shook her head.

"I can't tell you that yet. Don't you see? I can't bear to have him hurt you. It's so unnecessary. Please, tell him."

Bob looked down at the gray stone of the terrace.

"You're not just trying this on me? Saying that you care about me to make me tell?" he asked.

"No," she answered quickly. "Please, please, don't think that. It makes me sick. I hate all of it. I wouldn't do that, dear."

"All right," he answered. "I didn't think you would. I'm glad you wouldn't. Let's get this straight. You're working for what you believe in and I'm not trying to stop you. Well, I told you before — I don't know what it is you want on that plane, but I guess I've got the ace card. None of you are going to get it off this island. Either I get it or the British will. That's flat, isn't it?"

She was silent for a moment and their eyes met. Hers were deep and dark, like the colors on the sea, and she was not hurt or angry with him.

"I thought you'd say that," she said. "You're too honest not to."

"Then, let's forget it," Bob told her. "It doesn't do any good — that side of you or me — and the rest of it — Why, the rest of it is as out of place as the way Jameson looked. But let's talk about the rest of it. Suppose we did live here."

"Yes," she said, "let's talk about the rest of it. I knew I couldn't make you do anything else. That's why I love you, dear. There isn't anything left but to talk about something else, but it's awfully sad."

But she never told him why it was sad. Instead she was gay again, and they seemed to be entirely by themselves, although Oscar sat there watching them. She was asking him about the island and about the trees, and he told her about how he had bought the *Thistlewood*. He never remembered how long they sat there talking, seemingly alone together — until she said: —

"It's over now."

Oscar was on his feet listening. A voice was calling in the distance. It was Mr. Kingman's voice and Mrs. Kingman slipped down from the stone railing.

"Oscar!" Mr. Kingman was calling.

"I think they've found the plane." Mrs. Kingman sounded breathless and unsteady. "It's all over. He'll want the suitcase with the tools. Yes, they've found the plane."

CHAPTER XIV

OSCAR signaled Bob Bolles with the muzzle of his rifle and Bob walked along the terrace to the front of the house with Helen Kingman beside him. When he stood by the stone staircase that led from the front door and looked across the open space he saw that Mr. Kingman and Mr. Moto were far down the drive. When Mr. Kingman saw them he waved his hand and shouted again.

"Come on," he called. "Everybody come. The tools in the suitcase, Oscar. We've found it!" The case was where Oscar had put it when they had first ascended the steps, a heavy practical piece of luggage with Mr. Moto's cardboard suitcase and his raincoat just beside it.

"You pick it up," Oscar said, and Bob picked it up. Its weight told him that it was certainly full of metal. Then they walked across the open space toward Mr. Moto and Mr. Kingman. For a moment he wondered why Mr. Moto and Mr. Kingman were both there, when it would have been as easy for one of them to have gone to the house, but almost at once he understood the reason. Neither one of them could have left the other. They had evidently been scrambling through the undergrowth, for their clothes were stained with mud and grass and they both looked hot and weary. Mr. Kingman was paler and his face was drawn and thin. Mr. Moto's jaw was thrust a trifle forward and his eyes were beady and restless.

Mr. Kingman pushed back his sun helmet and rubbed his sleeve across his forehead.

"By Jove, it's hot work," he said, "as — as hot as hell. It's in that sugar factory — in a cellar on the end of it, under the old chimney arch. We've been crawling through those confounded vines. It is very annoying to think we had a full equipment, axes and everything, on the boat."

"Is it all there?" Mrs. Kingman asked. Mr. Kingman nodded.

"All there. Not crated. They must have broke her out to cut down on the weight when they carried her — one of the newer convoy pursuits — BCS–38–B. That is right, isn't it, Helen?"

"Yes," Mrs. Kingman said.

"All right," said Mr. Kingman briskly. "Then let's get going. You first, Bob. Let Oscar follow Bob, my dear. You'll see the path by the ruin, Bob. You'll see where we went through."

Then Mr. Moto raised his hand.

"Excuse me," Mr. Moto said. "May I ask a question, please? From the house where you left there was nothing on the sea?"

"*Nein,*" Oscar said, "it was all clear."

Mr. Moto glanced at his wrist-watch and looked happier.

"I think that is very nice," he said. "There should have been at least smoke by now. At least I do not think the American ship is coming." The gold in Mr. Moto's front teeth glistened. "Does it puzzle you, Mr. Bolles?"

"I never said a ship was coming," Bob Bolles told him.

"Thank you," Mr. Moto said. "Perhaps we may go now," and they walked along beneath the tall trees — Bob Bolles first, then Oscar, then Mrs. Kingman, and Mr. Moto and Mr. Kingman brought up the rear of the party, walking side by side. There was a path down by the ruins of the sugar factory which Mr. Moto and Mr. Kingman had broken through the brush, and Bob took it, stumbling over logs and stones. Mr. Kingman was right — it was fearfully hot in there.

The sugar factory had been built on the side of a hill and he could see the remains of its chimney through the brush. The floor of the factory had been supported by masonry arches and those arches were still intact, making shadowy caves. Before Bob Bolles saw the plane he saw a gap in the undergrowth toward the right which must have been certainly recently opened, but which now already was being choked with vines. The plane must have been wheeled up the avenue, and then through this opening to the sugar mill. A few steps farther on he saw its nose jutting out from beneath one of the arches, with a tarpaulin lashed tight over the engine. Although he had been prepared to see a plane there, it was startling to see it, with all its paint still almost new, with the transparent plastic of the hood still shining above the observer's and the pilot's seats — for all that new beautifully co-ordinated mechanism was so completely out of place beneath the stone ruin in the middle of the jungle. It stood there in the greenish shade as lonely and as fantastic as a surrealist picture. The ferns and vines, all the rank unconquerable vegetation of the tropics, were already creeping up to it and it was already stained by the weather.

It had been flown once on some testing field. Once it had been put through every possible strain and maneuver, but it would never fly again. The motor would never roar. The needles on the intricacy of its instrument panel would never give their signals. There was a musty smell of bats and decayed vegetation about it. It was a symbol of wasted effort and wasted ingenuity. Even without its wings, the fuselage was beautiful. It made Bob Bolles think of all the machinery and of all the hands that had worked on it, all for nothing, and it made him think of himself. He could see himself in the pilot's seat, warming up the motor; but like that plane, he would never fly again. The crashing of the undergrowth had died. As everyone stood around it in a half-circle, the only sound that Bob Bolles remembered afterwards was the rushing noise of water from a broken aqueduct above them which had once led to the mill. The water flowed in a little stream down by the old foundations and down the hill, half lost in a maze of undergrowth — a rotten place to leave a plane.

Bob had always had a flair for design and an instinct for line and mass. There were two things made by the hand of man which had always seemed to him infinitely superior to any other human achievement — a sailing ship and a plane. They both had the same miraculous quality of deceiving the normal blind forces of nature. A sailing ship could move into the wind which was blowing against her. A plane, by some amazing sort of mechanical sophistry, could make use of the normal forces of gravity and ultimately defy them. Like most of his old friends who had been educated in flying and who had a deep technical interest in their profession, Bob Bolles felt a selfless sort of mental exhilaration whenever he saw a plane. He almost forgot why he was there for a full minute, for he was like a naturalist examining a new species. His eye took in the line and the details of the construction. He was fitting those details into classifications based on his own experience. In a combat plane, of course, the accent was always on speed — speed in flight and speed in climbing. Such a machine would live or die by its margin of speed and maneuverability over its opponent. The plane looked fast, very fast, and yet there seemed to be nothing revolutionary or radical about the general design and nothing which he could see that was unusual about its method of construction. In fact, now that he looked at it, he had a puzzled sense of disappointment, for he had seen other models which were as good or better. Very little of the stressed duralumin skin was flash-riveted, just the nose section and the entering edge of the wings, and the split trailing edge flaps were mounted in the old-style manner. There was nothing in the body design worth worrying about, but the motor hidden beneath the tarpaulin might tell a different story. The weight of the suitcase dragging on his arm reminded him that he was still holding it and he set it down. When he did so, he saw that Mr. Moto and Mr. Kingman were both watching him as though they hoped to read something revealing in his expression.

"Well," Mr. Kingman said, "what do you think of her, Bob?"

"Just standing here," Bob Bolles answered, "I don't see anything new. She's good, but not too good."

Mr. Kingman nodded and Mr. Moto bobbed his head.

"Thank you," Mr. Moto said. "It so confirms Mr. Kingman's first impression. I think as we are as far as this we may as well consult Mrs. Kingman now, please."

Mr. Kingman nodded again and Mr. Moto bowed.

"If I may ask Mrs. Kingman, please," he said, "Mr. Kingman tells me that she has withheld her information up to this point which is very, very right, but I hope so very much you will feel free to tell us now, without our making trouble, Mrs. Kingman. We must know definitely now what new part it is, I think."

Mrs. Kingman sighed, as though she did not like the question.

"Do you want me to tell now, Mac?" she asked. "It seems to me — " She stopped and looked at Mr. Moto.

"My dear," Mr. Kingman said, "I know Mr. Moto's being here is embarrassing, but we have to get the

— the thing, whatever it is. We shall manage the other details later."

"Yes," Mr. Moto said, "later."

"You can't keep it to yourself any longer, my dear," Mr. Kingman said soothingly. "You understand that — don't you? We must know — right now."

"Yes," Mrs. Kingman said, and then she laughed.

"Please," Mr. Moto asked her, "what is so amusing?"

"It's only amusing," Mrs. Kingman answered, "because you none of you are fools. You must have had your own ideas all this time. It's on the motor, of course, a type of turbo supercharger. Get it off, and you can leave the rest of it."

Mr. Moto and Mr. Kingman listened, their attention completely absorbed by what she said, and the pause which followed when she had finished showed that they both had learned what they wished to know. It made an end of all the mystery. It placed all the cards upon the table. Somehow out there by the ruined sugar mill that modern jargon sounded strangely out of place. The words somehow contained an element of anticlimax and it seemed to Bob that a little of the anticlimax was reflected in Mr. Kingman's voice, although he could not be entirely sure.

"So that's it, is it?" Mr. Kingman said. "Something new in turbos?"

"Yes," Mrs. Kingman answered, "a new design."

Mr. Moto said nothing, but his glance traveled back again to the plane, and Bob Bolles saw that he was looking at the pilot's seat.

"Low octane gas, I suppose," Mr. Kingman said.

"Yes," Mrs. Kingman answered, "very low," and Mr. Kingman nodded.

"Pretty soon we'll be burning kerosene. Well, that's exactly what we need, what, Moto?"

"Yes," Mr. Moto answered carefully, "a variation of the Root invention, I suppose. Very, very interesting. The old superchargers are so difficult, I think."

Bob Bolles was thinking that the words were complicated, but not the principle behind the words, for all principles were simple. They were talking of a device for forcing a mixture of gasoline and air into the cylinders of an internal combustion engine, a device to increase the efficiency of the explosive mixture which made the engine go. Yet out of that simplicity came an enormous complication. It took you through a labyrinth of theories on which new engines were based. It meant the margin of speed, it meant the margin of climbing power, and the efficient use of low-grade fuel, for which the flying world was always struggling. Given a new design, it might mean almost anything. It was one of those secrets which, if known in time, might give a warring nation command of the air.

"All right," said Mr. Kingman, and he looked up at the sky through the trees. "Let's get over with this — this jawing. We've got some work ahead of us and it's getting late. Open up that suitcase, Bob. Here's where you come in." Bob Bolles turned his head from the plane.

"Where do I come in?" he asked.

"It's an idea of ours," Mr. Kingman said, "a — a cracking good idea." Mr. Moto coughed behind his hand.

"It is this way, please, Mr. Bolles," he said. "Mr. Kingman and I are both so suspicious." Mr. Moto paused to laugh politely. "I am so afraid Mr. Kingman would perhaps make some very serious mistake with the motor if he worked upon it and Mr. Kingman is so very much afraid that while he is working hard on the motor I might be tempted to — ah — liquidate the situation. Excuse me. It is so very funny."

"You said that before," Mr. Kingman said, and Bob Bolles noticed that his voice was growing edgy.

Mr. Moto placed his hand before his mouth and coughed again. "I have one little suggestion to make, please," he said. "We are getting so very near the end of our, ah, association and I have been so very, very tempted, so sorry several times that I have made the agreement. I have counted at least four opportunities when I might have ended matters."

"Don't be so sure," Mr. Kingman said. "Would you like to try it now?"

Mr. Moto's hand dropped carelessly into the right-hand pocket of his soiled white coat.

"It would be so foolish, don't you think," he said, "until we have finished the business here? I only suggest we get what we are looking for and walk back to the house upon the hill. Now if we should see a vessel coming — it is a matter which still worries me, please, for I am still not sure about Mr. Bolles — we may have to co-operate further."

"Go ahead," said Mr. Kingman. "Go ahead."

"But if everything is clear," Mr. Moto went on, "as I hope so very much it will be — " He paused and nodded at Mr. Kingman.

"Then the — the sky's the limit. Is that what you mean?" Mr. Kingman asked. "That's all right with me — when we get to the mainland."

"Thank you," Mr. Moto said. "I only wished that we understand everything so very clearly. Now, Mr. Bolles, you are to work on the plane. Take out the — ah — supercharger, please, and listen to me carefully. Mr. Kingman and I will watch everything you do. We will be so very interested. You must break nothing, make no mistake."

"He won't," Mr. Kingman said. "I know how to take a motor down. You understand, do you, Bob?"

Bob Bolles squared his shoulders.

"So sorry for you if you do not," Mr. Moto said before Bob could speak.

"I'll get it off for you," Bob Bolles said, "if you'll get that trained seal of yours to put down his gun and help."

"Seal?" said Mr. Kingman. "What trained seal?"

"Oscar," Bob Bolles said. "He can do everything but balance a ball on his nose."

"You shut your damned mouth," Oscar said and Mr. Kingman gave a shout of laughter.

"You're a — a good egg, Bob," he said. "Oscar, get the cover off that engine and do everything that Mr. Bolles says. I'll be watching. Get moving, Oscar."

"Trained seal," Mr. Moto said half to himself. "Why is he like a seal? I do not understand."

"I'll take Oscar's rifle, Mac," Mrs. Kingman said. It seemed to Bob Bolles that a shade of perplexity crossed Mr. Kingman's face.

"What?" he said. "What's that, Helen?"

"I just said I could hold Oscar's rifle, Mac," Mrs. Kingman said.

"Why, of course, my dear," Mr. Kingman answered. "Unload it, Oscar, and give it to Mrs. Kingman. I mean nothing personal, oh no, of course not. It's just in case you might do something you'd be sorry for. Get the cover off, Oscar. Open up those tools, Bob."

Bob Bolles opened the case. It was beautifully fitted with a set of tools, socket wrenches of all sizes, a kit that any ground mechanic would have been proud of.

"Hello," Bob said. "It's made in Germany!"

"Don't talk," Mr. Kingman told him. "Get to work."

Oscar had ripped the tarpaulin off the engine and Bob picked up the tools. He was familiar enough with the business, for he had been through it often and he had seen it done by others many times. While he and Oscar dragged up some stones from which to make a platform on which to work and when he asked Oscar for a hammer and handed Oscar another screw or nut, most of his actions were mechanical. After he had unfastened the quick detachable latches and had opened the engine compartment cowling, the whole maze of mechanism was exposed behind the cylinders. The whole space up to the fire wall, protecting the pilot's compartment, was criss-crossed with braces, wiring, piping, fuel pumps and generators. He began dismantling these obstructions, groping through the center of the mass for the turbo supercharger. It was not an easy job, for the tools in that German kit were in metric sizes, always a little too tight or too loose. He looked down once, from where he was standing, at Mr. Kingman.

"Too bad you didn't bring American tools," he said.

"There was every reason why this engine should be metric," Mr. Kingman answered. "The plane was for the French. These confounded English inches — someday the whole world will be on the metric system."

"I suppose it will," Bob said, "if boys like you run it," and he searched among the tools for a ratchet-head, socket end-wrench.

"Just get it out," said Mr. Kingman. "Get it out."

Perspiration was streaming into Bob Bolles's eyes and his face and shirt were smeared with grease.

"He does well, I think," he heard Mr. Moto say.

"Yes," Mr. Kingman said, "he knows his job. I do not like liquid cooling."

"Fetch that hammer, Oscar," Bob Bolles called, and if they said anything further he did not hear it for a while. The pipes and the wires were cleared and the turbo supercharger was in front of him.

He did not hear their voices, because he was too much concerned with a dull, bewildered surprise of his own. It was modern, but he had seen the whole thing before. It was all like a book or a picture he had known; that piece of mechanism which they wanted had already been shipped across the water in hundreds of other engines. There was something wrong somewhere. He knew it, because he had examined the very type before. There it was — heavy and bulky, about the size of a man's hatbox. He could see the outlines of the twin housing and the intercooler. The finish was already scorched and chipped and scaling from the heat of the test runs. If they wanted that supercharger, they were mistaken. He knew they were mistaken. If they wanted it, he was face to face with a secret he must keep. There was something else in that plane — certainly something else. Still holding the wrench, Bob looked down at Mr. Kingman and rubbed the perspiration from his eyes.

"Well, there it is," he said. "Do you want to see it?"

"We'll see it when it's off," Mr. Kingman said.

Bob looked down at the octagonal bolts which were holding it. There was certainly something else, and it was not there in the engine. There was something which they did not know about. He turned his head away from them, hoping they would not see any change in his expression.

"This end-wrench keeps slipping," he said. "Do you mind if I look in the cockpit for a minute?"

"What for? What is it you want?" Mr. Kingman asked.

"There ought to be some tools," Bob Bolles said. "If I could get an end-wrench that fits — "

"Very well," Mr. Kingman said, "but hurry, you understand?"

Bob Bolles climbed slowly into the cockpit. He

knew that they were watching him and he could not stay there long. His legs felt weak and watery. Since it was not in the engine, it would be on the instrument board, as sure as fate. He would only have a minute to look at the complexity of the dials, just a minute, as he peered down inside, but it did not take a minute to see it. His eye was trained so that he saw it almost instantly. He made an effort to keep his face immobile and not to stare too hard. Right there in the cockpit was the end of everything, a secret that was worth dying for, and they must not know it. It was there by the radio, something which he had heard talk of, but which he did not know existed. When he saw it, his mind was saying: —

"*That's it. Don't let them know.*"

If he had had a hammer, he could have smashed it, but he did not have a hammer. If he could get his hand on something — His mind was still speaking to him. The words were inside his head, just as though someone else were speaking: —

"*Night combat. Beam 21 A.*"

That plane could fight by night as well as it could by daylight. You did not need eyes to point its guns. Its eyes were in front of him, right there on the panel.

"Never mind that wrench," Mr. Kingman said. "Do what you can with the one you've got. It's getting late."

"Just give me a minute, won't you?" Bob Bolles asked. It was there — right in front of him. He could have smashed it, if he had only had a hammer.

"No," Mr. Kingman said, "get out of there. It's getting late."

"Wait," Mr. Moto said. "Perhaps Mr. Bolles has found something."

"Yes, I have," Bob answered, and he picked up a piece of cotton waste and wiped his face with it. "This is something I've been wanting."

"Come on," Mr. Kingman said. "Get out of there. We're waiting."

Then he was back at the engine again, straining at the bolts, and he remembered that Mr. Kingman was telling him to hurry. He could understand their impatience, because the blue of the sky was growing deeper and the shadows were growing longer. They wanted to be finished before the quick black curtain of the tropical night came down on them. But nothing mattered, so long as no one understood the meaning of those dials in the cockpit. He was thinking of all the talk about a fighting plane which could follow every motion of the enemy in the dark. He had heard of it — and now he had seen it. It would make night bombing as dangerous as day bombing. He had heard of it, without believing it.

"All right," he said. "Give me a hand, Oscar."

The turbo was heavy. He and Oscar carried it down between them and set it carefully on the ground, a chunky, unimpressive object, which no one unfamiliar with engines could have identified. They stood in a little group looking at it, while Bob Bolles wiped the grease from his face and hands. He thought they would know, but apparently they did not, for both Mr. Moto and Mr. Kingman seemed entirely satisfied, and all their attention was focused upon the thing on the ground.

"Very nice," said Mr. Moto. "Thank you so much, Mr. Bolles."

"Yes," said Mr. Kingman, "most ingenious, entirely a new design. Well, there's no use waiting any longer."

"No," said Mr. Moto, "none at all."

Then Bob's eyes met Mrs. Kingman's. It occurred to him that he must be looking very badly — his shirt nothing more than a wet rag, his face a smear of grease.

"Oscar," Mr. Kingman said, "cut up the tarpaulin and swing that thing in it. Mr. Bolles can carry it." And a minute or two later Bob had the thing, in a rude sack over his shoulder.

"It is so necessary to get back," Mr. Moto said. "I should like to see if the horizon is clear."

"All right," said Mr. Kingman. "We can leave the tools. Come ahead, Bob."

But Mr. Moto still hesitated as though something careless in their haste disturbed his conscientious sense of order and his hesitation seemed to annoy Mr. Kingman.

"What is it now?" Mr. Kingman asked impatiently. "You said we ought to hurry."

"So sorry," Mr. Moto said. "Are you so very sure we have everything?"

Mr. Kingman's voice was hearty and positive.

"There isn't another damned thing here," he said, "that isn't on any other ship. That's so, isn't it, Helen?"

"Do you think we'd come away out here and leave what we want?" Mrs. Kingman asked Mr. Moto. "Of course we have everything."

"But the controls, please," Mr. Moto said, "the instruments."

"Really, Mr. Moto," Mrs. Kingman told him, "you're not being very sensible. Our Intelligence has been over every specification."

"It was only a question," Mr. Moto said. "So glad to take your word. Do you agree with them, Mr. Bolles?"

"Yes," Bob Bolles said, "absolutely. There's nothing novel about the design or the equipment. And now I'd like to ask, since you've got the supercharger, what else do you want with me?"

His question appeared to make them forget the plane. It met with a moment's embarrassed sort of silence.

"Keep — keep your shirt on," Mr. Kingman said. "You're going back with us to the house. We'll take up the matter of the boat next."

It was the beginning of sunset when they reached the old avenue again. They walked back in the same order as before, except that Mrs. Kingman walked beside him. Bob Bolles glanced over his shoulder. Oscar was just behind them, his rifle ready, and some paces farther back came Mr. Kingman and Mr. Moto. The sky was growing red with the setting sun and there were purple colors in the hills, now that the bright glare of the day was going.

"Look at the sky," Mrs. Kingman said. "It's growing pink like wine and water. When I was a little girl — "

"You lived on Park Avenue, didn't you?" Bob Bolles said.

"No," Mrs. Kingman answered, "perhaps I'll tell you sometime. When I was a little girl my father would put a spoonful of wine in my water glass. The color was just like the sky. Bob — "

"What?" Bob Bolles said, because she seemed to be waiting for him to say something.

"You should learn to live in the present, always in

the present, like the rest of us. Just the moment — nothing more."

"I've got a good deal to think about," Bob Bolles said.

"Don't," she told him. "Think about the sky."

He was trying to hear what Mr. Kingman and Mr. Moto were saying.

"Heigh-ho," he heard Mr. Kingman humming, ". . . home from work we go."

They were nearly at the top of the rising ground. The walls of the ruined manor house, stark against the sky in front of them, were also changing color with the sunset, and then the sea and the harbor lay below them. There was nothing in the harbor, nothing on the horizon.

"Very well," Mr. Moto said. "I am so very much relieved. I do not think that we will be disturbed until tomorrow."

"Yes," said Mr. Kingman slowly, "it looks all — hunky-dory. It's about time that we — we simplified matters, isn't it, Moto?"

"Yes," said Mr. Moto softly, "I agree to that."

CHAPTER XV

"ALL RIGHT," Mr. Kingman said. "Oscar, light up a little fire inside there and put some coffee on. We'll all do better with a little wine and coffee and chicken."

Oscar looked at Mr. Kingman questioningly and Mr. Kingman nodded.

"It's all right, Oscar," he said. "Bob, you can set that thing down now, gently, very gently. It's too heavy to be stolen. It will be safe right here."

Oscar crossed the terrace and disappeared through one of the gaping windows inside the house and Bob Bolles set down the canvas bundle he had been carrying. Although the weight was off his shoulders, his muscles still ached and his back was still bent and all at once he felt deathly tired. He could see that the sun was dropping fast. There would be a few minutes of twilight and then it would be dark.

"Now," Mr. Kingman said, and Mr. Kingman did not look tired at all, "it looks as though we must begin to simplify matters. You had your chance to talk to

Bob, Helen. Did you get any satisfaction out of him?"

There was no doubt what Mr. Kingman meant, although his voice did not show it; and there was no doubt that Mrs. Kingman understood, because she looked deathly ill.

"Answer me, Helen," Mr. Kingman said. "Can he get the boat back?"

But Mr. Moto answered before she could speak and his voice was as smooth as silk.

"There is no need for Mrs. Kingman to answer, please," he said. "We no longer have necessity for Mr. Bolles, I am so very much afraid. So sorry, when he has been so helpful. Yes, the boat will come back, when a fire has been built upon the beach."

Something seemed to catch Bob Bolles by the throat. He never thought that it was fear as much as blank astonishment that Mr. Moto seemed to know almost everything. He could not imagine how Mr. Moto could have guessed it.

"What the devil!" Mr. Kingman said. "Did he tell you, Moto?"

Mr. Moto looked childishly pleased and he gave one of his short artificial laughs.

"Oh, no, please," he said. "When your little boat came in I was so interested to watch. I saw a black man slide from her into the water and swim to land. It did not seem to me correct. When he came to shore I stopped him. That was all. It was not necessary to

234

be rough. He was so very much afraid. He told me that he was to take the boat away. Oh, yes, he told me everything."

"Why the devil didn't you tell us sooner?" Mr. Kingman asked.

Mr. Moto's whole face broke into a happy smile.

"So many things, Mr. Kingman," he said, "that I do not tell until necessary. Please, I wish so much to make use of Mr. Bolles as long as possible."

"Well," said Mr. Kingman, "that's about all we need of him, isn't it?"

"Yes," Mr. Moto answered, "I am so afraid I really think so."

Mr. Kingman looked troubled and Bob could almost believe that Mr. Kingman did not like any of it.

"It's a little — tough," he said. "You — know too much. Anything you want to say, Bob?"

When Bob Bolles thought of it, there seemed to be absolutely nothing. He was thinking of the plane by the sugar mill. He would have liked to have a chance of getting to the plane again, but there was no chance. They had used him. They had driven him like a horse, until they were finished with him.

"No," he said; "to hell with the whole lot of you!"

But Mr. Kingman still was troubled. His whole manner was kindly, almost apologetic.

"It is only that there are too many of us here, Bob," he said. "It's only you've got yourself into a damned dirty game, and you're in the way. I do hope you see it, Bob. Oh, well, let's have some coffee and a bite to eat." Mr. Kingman slapped his hand on Bob Bolles's shoulder. "There's nothing personal, you know, old man. Everybody draws — his number sometime. You'll feel better with a good hot cup of coffee."

But there was something personal, and Bob Bolles knew it. All Mr. Kingman's solicitude was a slimy sort of mockery. He knew that Mr. Kingman was enjoying himself. He remembered Mr. Kingman's look when he had driven the butt of his rifle into Inspector Jameson.

"I'd feel better if you'd put that rifle down," Bob said. "Maybe we could talk a few personalities."

Mr. Kingman moved a step nearer to him and looked him up and down appraisingly.

"I'm not — not yellow," Mr. Kingman said. "That's the word, isn't it? I'd like to oblige you really, old man, if I didn't have any other business. I'm sorry I can't use you on your boat. We have to make the best of that black boy of yours. You'll sail her, won't you, Moto?"

"Yes," Mr. Moto said, "oh, yes. So sorry we can manage without Mr. Bolles."

"Yes, Bob," said Mr. Kingman, "everybody's sorry — and Helen will be particularly, won't you, my dear?"

Mrs. Kingman did not answer.

"Yes, Helen will be particularly sorry," Mr. Kingman said. "Now come inside. Some coffee will do you good. You'll need it for what's coming, won't he, Oscar?"

Mr. Moto coughed behind his hand.

"Excuse, please," he said. "I think, ah, Mr. Kingman, that you are not being polite. I ask you to be polite. Mr. Bolles behaves like a Japanese gentleman."

"Polite?" Mr. Kingman answered. "Why, damn your eyes, don't you hear me telling him I'm sorry? Walk ahead, Bob. Gentlemen first. Oscar's boiling up the coffee."

They walked inside the roofless house. Oscar had already kindled a fire in a corner and had piled stones around it and had placed the coffeepot on the stones. Inspector Jameson was propped against a pile of rubbish, almost exactly where they had left him.

"Ah," said Mr. Kingman, "not able to break loose, were you? Take his gag out, Oscar. Let's hear the latest news from the British Empire. How is it with you, my dear fellow?"

Anyone could see that it was not well at all with Inspector Jameson. He made an effort to speak, but he could only make a few inarticulate sounds. Mr. Kingman shook his finger at him.

"Careful," he said. "Don't forget anything you say

may be used against you. How about a little water, old chap? Oscar, give me a cup of water."

Mr. Kingman held the cup in front of Inspector Jameson and the big man leaned toward it.

"Thirsty, yes?" said Mr. Kingman. "There you are," and he tossed the contents into Inspector Jameson's face. "Put the gag back, Oscar," he went on.

Mr. Moto coughed again.

"Please," he said, "I think that is enough."

"Why," said Mr. Kingman, "that's pretty. I thought you Japs were all — all hard-boiled. Well, here comes the coffee. Let's sit down again," and Mr. Kingman waved toward the improvised stone table. "Open up the wine, Oscar. Just a farewell toast for Bob here. You see, after supper, Bob, I'm going to ask you to go."

"Where?" Bob asked.

"Just out," said Mr. Kingman, "anywhere, if — if you can make it."

"Mac," Mrs. Kingman began, and she stopped.

"It's no good speaking about it, my dear," Mr. Kingman said. "You know as well as I do that the — the party must break up. A little more coffee, Bob?"

"No, thanks," Bob Bolles answered.

"Mac," Mrs. Kingman began again, "I can't sit here — "

"My dear," said Mr. Kingman, "you don't have

to. You can walk outside for a while. The wind is rising, isn't it?"

Mr. Kingman looked up through the gaping roof. The wind was sighing about the walls and all the light was out of the sky by then and the stars were coming out. The darkness was closing around them, except for the circle of light from the little fire where Oscar had boiled the coffee, so that all their faces were in shadow.

"Oscar," said Mr. Kingman, "did you bring candles?"

"*Ja,*" Oscar said, "I have light."

Oscar pulled a folding candle lantern from the picnic hamper and lighted it and set it on the stone around which they were sitting.

"Very pretty," Mr. Moto said. "The wind does not blow it. Candlelight is so very interesting."

"Do you know," Mr. Kingman said, "we've all had quite — quite a day? Oscar, have you any cards?"

"*Ja,*" Oscar said, from the shadows near the fire, "I have brought a pack."

"How about a hand of bridge?" Mr. Kingman said. "Bob's an — an A 1 player."

"That would be very nice," Mr. Moto said. "There should be time for one hand, I think." Oscar handed Mr. Kingman the cards.

"As long as there are four of us," Mr. Kingman

239

said, "the stone is a little rough, but it will do. Shall we cut for deal?"

Suddenly Mrs. Kingman's voice was harsh and broken.

"You coward," she cried.

"Why, my dear," Mr. Kingman said, "this isn't like you!"

"Making him play bridge!" Mrs. Kingman said.

"Helen," Mr. Kingman said, "please sit down and pick up your cards. It isn't like you."

Mr. Moto picked up his cards. "I should like to say, please," Mr. Moto said, "that Mr. Bolles is very nice."

"He is," Mr. Kingman said heartily, "a — a jolly good fellow."

Bob Bolles looked across at him. Mr. Kingman was his partner. Mr. Kingman still kept one hand on his rifle.

"One diamond, please," Mr. Moto said.

When the bidding came to Bob Bolles he made it a spade. Then he looked up and saw that Oscar had gone. They passed when Bob Bolles bid four spades. Mr. Kingman laid down the dummy and Bob Bolles began to play the hand. It was difficult to keep his mind on the cards, but he played them. He made four spades and one over.

"Well," he said, "that's that," and he stood up and

everyone else stood up. Mr. Moto had dropped his right hand into his pocket.

"Bob," Mr. Kingman said, "your sense of cards is excellent."

"Such a nice hand," Mr. Moto said, "and to make the three of diamonds good — so very nice."

"Hélène," Mr. Kingman said, "you must be tired. Perhaps a little walk in the air — "

She did not look at any of them. She brushed by Bob Bolles without looking at him and half walked, half ran out into the darkness.

"Well, Bob," Mr. Kingman said after a moment, but his eyes never left Mr. Moto. "Well, the party's over. I guess you'd better be going."

"You mean, you're going to let me out of here?" Bob Bolles asked. "Why?"

"Never mind why," Mr. Kingman answered. "You're free to go anywhere now."

"And what are you two boys going to do?" Bob Bolles asked.

"Oh, Mr. Bolles," said Mr. Moto, "he will talk. I am happy to have met you, Mr. Bolles."

"All right," Bob Bolles answered. "Well, so long." That old desire came over him, that they must not think he was afraid. "Maybe I'll be seeing you."

The tall window that opened out on the terrace was just in front of them. It framed the blackness of the world outside, a darkness that was accentuated by the candle lantern and the flickering little fire in the space where Mr. Moto and Mr. Kingman were standing. When Bob stepped through that window out to the terrace, whether he moved fast or slow, his whole figure would be outlined by the light behind him, and Oscar was out there on the terrace. Mr. Kingman had said that he was free to go anywhere, but Bob Bolles did not believe it. He knew too much for them to permit him to walk away. Yet he had to move, and the prospect of the black night outside was worse than anything he had imagined, because for a certain space of time he would be absolutely helpless. As he stepped slowly toward the window, he must have been weighing all the facts and his perceptions were very clear. If he could get out of the circumference of light he might have a chance. He might be able to dart around a corner, but Oscar would not be such a fool as to let him have that chance — he would get him while he was in the light.

CHAPTER XVI

BOB BOLLES took another step. One more and he would be outside. His instinct was to bend double and to make a dash for it, and it was all he could do to control that instinct. He did so, because his common sense told him that the only difference would be that he would be killed running instead of walking. He felt a cold spasm of unadulterated fear, but if he was to be finished anyway, there was no use having them realize that he had been afraid. He did not even want to hesitate. He shrugged his shoulders and stepped from the light into the dark. His whole body was braced and waiting. His eyes were unaccustomed to the dark, so for a second everything seemed pitch-black, but nothing happened. Mechanically he took another step, and nothing happened. He could feel himself breathing in sharp, hard breaths. The sea breeze struck his face and he could hear the wind in the treetops on the slope below the clearing. He could see the outline of the stone railing of the terrace. All the shapes and shadows were illuminated by the stars — a fantastic, monotonous world of light and shade. He had stepped out of the light of the house and he was in the shadow and free from it.

His first sensation was an utter incredulity and then his knees were shaking and then he was filled with panic-stricken desire — to get out of there, to get as far away as possible. The terrace railing was not thirty feet in front of him, dimly white in the starlight. His one desire was to get to the railing and to leap over it and go. He must have covered half the distance to it in that sort of cloudy progress which one connects with a bad dream, with all his thought focused on reaching the railing, when he saw Mrs. Kingman. She must have stepped from the shadow of the house, but he was not sure. At any rate, she was in front of him, diagonally to his left. She was waving her arm at him, gesturing to him to turn. He had half turned his head when he heard a soft thudding footfall behind him and saw Oscar, a whitish crouching shape. He even had time to see that Oscar was holding a rope in his hands, but he did not have time to turn. He hardly had time to brace himself before Oscar had sprung at him and had landed with all his force upon his back. Yet even in that instant he understood — he was to be garroted, strangled with the rope. He would have been done for, if he had not turned his head. As it was, his body was thrown forward beneath the impact of Oscar's momentum, but he kept his feet. He had raised his hand, he had grasped Oscar by the arm. His right hand was holding the back of Oscar's neck, and then with a spasmodic lunge he had thrown Oscar from him. Oscar was catapulting through space, and then he landed head first, crash, against the stone railing.

When he analyzed it afterwards, Bob could see that some hideous coincidence had made every factor right — Oscar's momentum, his own forward lunge, the instinctive backward grasping of his arms — everything had fitted into that result; but Bob Bolles did not think of it then. All he saw was Oscar's bulk, crumpled against the railing. He heard Oscar breathing in long snoring gasps, and then he heard Mr. Kingman's voice from the house behind him.

"There it goes," he heard Mr. Kingman say. "Oscar's very handy. Good-by, Mr. Bolles."

At least he thought that he had heard Mr. Kingman say it, but he was never wholly sure, for Mrs. Kingman had snatched his hand. She was pulling him after her across the terrace down the broad stone steps. They were running and he saw that she was holding a long knife in her other hand.

"Hurry," she gasped, "over to the trees!" And she ran beside him across the clearing from the house.

He seemed to feel no reaction and no reality until

they were beneath the shadow of the trees. He stopped there and she leaned against him, clinging to him, fighting for her breath.

"His head — " she gasped.

"Yes," Bob said, "I know." The pulses in his ears and throat were pounding, but he could still hear that crash of Oscar's head against the stones and the snoring sound of Oscar's breathing.

"I was going to help you," he heard her say. "The knife — I did not need to help."

He stared dully at the knife in her hand. He could see the blade glitter in the dark.

"Thank God!" she said. "Kiss me. I love you so."

It still was like a dream, but it did not seem strange when he kissed her. Then she drew away from him and looked back at the house. He could see the black walls against the sky and the light of the candle lantern, and as he looked, he heard Mr. Kingman's voice.

"Oscar," he heard Mr. Kingman call, "Oscar!"

"They will shoot," Mrs. Kingman whispered. "Wait! Where are you going?" She snatched at his arm and held him. Her hand was very strong.

"I'm getting to that plane," he said. "It wasn't that turbo and you know it, and I'll bet Mac knew it too. Let go of me!" But she leaned against him again, still holding fast to his wrist. He heard the sharp intake of her breath and then she was speaking very quickly.

"Oh, God," she said, "don't do that, please! Because I can't let you, my dear. Don't you see I really can't? Of course Mac knew it. But the Japanese, he doesn't know."

He tried to push her away from him gently, but she still clung to him.

"No, my dear," she was saying, "not that. Please, not that! You mustn't. It's what I came here for. It's mine — Bob, please! I love you so."

Then a sound from the house made him start, although he must have been ready for it. It was the sharp crack of a rifle shot, and a second shot followed it almost simultaneously, and then before he could speak, another.

"You see," he heard her say, "the Japanese — he's killed him! Bob, dear, he doesn't know. It's mine!"

Then he wrenched his arm away from her.

"Oh, no, it isn't," he said. "I'm getting back to that plane!"

"Bob," she said, "Bob, please!" And her voice choked in a sob, and then she thrust the knife at him. He saw it coming in a sickening, leaden instant, and even in that instant he must have been ready. He must have known that she would do it, for he beat her arm aside with his open palm, snatched at her wrist and wrenched the knife from her hand.

"By God," he said, "you're quite a girl!" And then he turned and ran.

Yes, she was quite a girl. Just as he began to run he heard Mr. Moto's voice, thin and clear, calling from the house.

"Oh, Mrs. Kingman, it is quite all right," he heard Mr. Moto calling. "But where is Mr. Bolles?"

He looked over his shoulder once as he ran down the grassy avenue and he could see the faint flicker of light through the gaping windows of the ruined house. It was faint enough to be as feeble and ghost-like as the lights of the will-o'-the-wisp in some folk tale. His eyes were accustomed to the starlight so that he saw the walls of the sugar house against the sky at the left and he was even able to distinguish the gap in the brush where they had beaten the path toward it that afternoon. He ran along it, stumbling, falling and picking himself up again.

"By God," he heard himself saying again, "you're quite a girl!"

But it was like them, like the whole crew of them. It was ugly, but a part of it was clear. That work on the plane had been for Mr. Moto's benefit, for neither she nor Kingman could want him to know what it was they wanted. They had worked together, but she had been waiting all the time. He remembered when she had asked to take Oscar's rifle. She must have been ready to finish it off right then and to give Mr. Moto the supercharger and to let him go. Yes, she was quite a girl, and she had said again she loved him —

He paused in the clearing by the sugar mill and listened, but he knew it was no time for listening. Then his foot struck against the case of tools. Of course Mr. Kingman had left them there, because at his convenience he was coming back. Then Bob was on his knees, fumbling for a hammer. Then he was scrambling into the cockpit. He knew where it was, even in the dark, but even when he smashed it he was thinking. He was thinking that they had been too kind to him — or perhaps too clever. It would have been better for the lot of them if they had shot him that morning near the beach.

It was over, but it was not entirely finished. He left the plane and walked back toward the house. He had smashed the mechanism in the cockpit beyond any conceivable possibility of reconstruction. They were washed up, they were through.

CHAPTER XVII

HE WAS never able to judge the actual time it had taken him to reach the plane and to return, but it must have been shorter than he had thought, for when he arrived at the head of the avenue the light was still inside the house. But when he walked into the opening the light moved. Someone was carrying the lantern out to the terrace. He heard voices and he saw two figures walking forward to the steps, and then they must have seen him, for he heard Mrs. Kingman say: —

"There he is now. He was out there in the trees." And then he heard Mr. Moto's voice calling to him: —

"Come toward us, Mr. Bolles. No fear of anything any longer, please."

Then as he came nearer, he saw that Mrs. Kingman was coming down the steps, carrying the lantern, and that Mr. Moto was beside her. His Panama hat was pulled over his eyes and his left arm was in a sling, made from one of the picnic napkins, and his right hand was in his pocket.

"It's all right," Mrs. Kingman said. "You don't have to hide any longer."

She looked ill and very tired, but she was smiling at him and there was no trace of resentment in her voice. Instead there was a definite ring to it, as though she wanted to make something clear to him, and he understood it. She was telling him as plainly as though she had spoken that she did not want Mr. Moto to know where he had been. He saw Mr. Moto's eyes beneath the shadow of his hat brim, fixed upon him steadily.

"You were hiding, Mr. Bolles?" Mr. Moto asked.

"What else do you think I'd be doing?" Bob asked back. "Running around in the woods for exercise? All I wanted was to get out from under."

"Get out from under," Mr. Moto said. "So nice the way you say things, Mr. Bolles."

"Where is Kingman?" Bob Bolles asked.

There was a second's silence and Bob Bolles heard the wind sigh past the corners of the house and he heard Mr. Moto clear his throat.

"So sorry," Mr. Moto said. "Mr. Kingman is not with us any more."

Mr. Moto's delicacy made it sound more gruesome and when Bob Bolles did not answer, Mr. Moto continued still more delicately.

"So sorry that it was of course so necessary. He was

251

so nice and so much quicker with his rifle than I thought. So quick, my first — ah — shot I am sorry was a little wild. He felt nothing after the second, I am so very, very sure. Yes, for what he was, he was very, very nice. So nice the way he laughed, did you not think so, Mrs. Kingman?"

"No," Mrs. Kingman said, and her voice sounded harsh and strained. "I hated it."

Bob Bolles started to speak and stopped.

"Oscar," he began, "is Oscar — "

Mr. Moto's voice cut his own voice off, as he hesitated. It sounded serene and final, devoid of passion or regret.

"He is not with us any more."

"You mean," Bob said, and it made him feel sick, "you mean I killed him?"

"Yes," said Mr. Moto gently. "His skull was broken, Mr. Bolles. It saved me so much trouble."

"My God — " Bob Bolles began, and he stopped again. He did not like to admit it, but as he watched Mrs. Kingman and Mr. Moto he felt himself shiver.

"You may see them if you like," Mr. Moto said. "They are both up there. Please, it was not bad for either of them."

"Of course he does not want to see them," Mrs. Kingman said sharply. "Let's leave here now." But Bob Bolles still stood facing them.

"But what about Jameson?" he asked. "He isn't — "

Mr. Moto shook his head.

"No, the Englishman is well. Still at the house. So uncomfortable for him, I am afraid. A little sick, but he is well." Mr. Moto did not appear conscious of the contradiction, and perhaps it was not a contradiction either.

"Where I come from human life is not held so dear perhaps. So many worse things than dying. But I do not like to hurt people, Mr. Bolles, unless it is so very necessary. I hope so very much you will believe me. That is why the Englishman is so very well, and you too, Mr. Bolles."

"Don't make me laugh," Bob said harshly. "You were going to kill me like a dog this morning by the beach."

"Yes," said Mr. Moto gravely, "that was true. So happy it is different now."

"And you didn't lift a finger this evening," Bob said. "Don't make me laugh."

"So sorry," Mr. Moto answered and he sounded almost hurt. "You do not understand me, please. Mrs. Kingman knows me so much better. I try so hard to be honorable. This evening I arranged myself to help you. I gave the knife to Mrs. Kingman. She was so very anxious for you. You were not an obstacle to

253

me any more. I like you very much. I wish we might be friends."

"We're not going to be friends," Bob said, "if you leave Jameson up there. I'll untie him if you won't."

"Wait." Mr. Moto moved his pistol urgently. "He will stay up there, please."

"Yes, Bob," said Mrs. Kingman. "Listen to Mr. Moto. He's very sensible and it's all arranged."

"He will stay, please," Mr. Moto said, "because it is the best place for him. He understands because he is reasonable and, for an Englishman, he is quite polite. We have even tried to make him comfortable. He has sent you his regards. He says it will be all right for you in Kingston. His people will find him tomorrow. This is no pleasure for any of us, please. Mrs. Kingman and I have reached an understanding and arrangement. I am so very glad. We began to understand each other down on the beach this morning."

"How did you do that?" Bob asked. "You never spoke to her." Mr. Moto's gold teeth glistened in the candlelight.

"So very simple," he said. "A gesture and a glance. This morning when I appeared the look was so plain on Mrs. Kingman's face. She hoped so very much that I would eliminate Mr. Kingman. It was more simple after that."

Mrs. Kingman stood holding the lantern and Bob

saw that she was looking at him, half defiantly, half beseechingly.

"Of course it's hard for you to understand, my dear," she said, "because you will never be like any of us. So much of this must have seemed to you aimless and you could never see behind the curtain. We can be truthful now because there is nothing left to hide. I could not get away from Mac — not from the moment he met me in New York. I could not trust him. I always thought that he would turn on me when he found out what I knew and use it for himself, and I was right, you know."

"Then, why did you work with him?" Bob asked.

"Because he was completely logical," she answered. "Even Charles Durant in New York, and he was one of our best men, went over Mac's credentials and advised that it was all right. But something must have turned up later. Charles must have suspected something. I knew that Mac was out for himself when I heard that Charles had come to Kingston. You told me — you remember."

She stopped, but her eyes were telling him that she was speaking the truth. Both she and Mr. Moto seemed anxious to explain. He could imagine them at some later time sitting together composedly and talking it all over.

"Poor Charles," she said. "All of us must go sometime, but Charles was very kind to me. He was one of our best men."

"Oh, a very nice man," Mr. Moto said helpfully. "We once exchanged shots in Saigon in the dark, but he was very nice. It was so careless of Mr. Kingman not to make it surely look like suicide. And, please, Mr. Bolles, I wish that you would like us. Mrs. Kingman has been very brave. I have so very much respect."

"Yes," Bob said, "I know she's brave."

"This evening at sunset I gave her the knife," Mr. Moto went on. "When Oscar attacked you it was the opportunity we both were looking for. She was to — ah — deal with Oscar when he was dealing with you, Mr. Bolles, and Mr. Kingman — that was my responsibility."

"Bob," she said, "I wouldn't have let him kill you."

Mr. Moto laughed in that polite nervous way of his. There was no humor in it, but it was his way of making matters easier.

"And now it is all arranged. No more little unpleasantness. Mrs. Kingman has been sensible enough to surrender the piece of machinery to me. It still lies by the house, but will be collected in the morning. No need to stand here longer. I am going with you and Mrs. Kingman to the beach. We shall light a fire and I shall be so happy to permit you and Mrs. Kingman to go. Your schooner will be in by dawn, I hope. Just you and Mrs. Kingman, please. I shall not go with you."

And then Bob understood why it was better not to mention his visit to the plane.

"You're not going with us?" Bob asked. "What are you going to do?"

"I have already made arrangements, thank you," Mr. Moto said. "There is a wireless in my suitcase — a message to friends on the mainland. They will be coming in the morning in a plane. I would prefer you not to be here. It might be so embarrassing. We shall go to the beach now and I think you are very lucky, Mr. Bolles."

"Yes," Bob said, and he spoke with deep conviction, "I'm mighty lucky."

CHAPTER XVIII

Mrs. KINGMAN was speaking.

"Look," she said, "the moon is coming up! It will be moonlight on the beach. I love it in the moonlight."

And Bob Bolles could almost believe that she had put it all away from her and that it was all forgotten. It was monstrous, but there was nothing monstrous in what she said. She looked different again — young again and beautiful.

Bob Bolles had admired moonlight often enough himself, but when the moon was up that night its light had an uncanny, revealing quality which brought out all sorts of facts which had been hidden by the sun. He had often thought that the moon on tropical waters signified peace and good will and coolness after the heat of the day, but that night the moonlight only made him restless and wide-awake. He kept thinking, as they walked to the beach in silence, that the house behind them would be bathed in a sort of deadly whiteness. Ghosts would already be walking up there by the house. The path in front of them was a sort of shadowy black and white and the moon was drawing all the warmth from the earth, making the shadows dank and cold. The moon made Mr. Moto's face icily serene. He was wounded, but he smiled politely, so genially that Bob believed his shoulder was giving him pain.

"Oh, yes," said Mr. Moto, "I always think the moon is very, very nice."

It made Bob Bolles wonder what he was really thinking, whether everything in Mr. Moto's world was either very nice or very serious and whether Mr. Moto was ever anything but very glad or very sorry. Mr. Moto's reactions could not always be as simple as that, but he was completely sure of himself, and sure of what he wished to do. He must have learned it from his way of life, and suddenly Bob Bolles realized that he had learned it too. Everything was in a new perspective. His whole sense of values was different, so changed that he was like a different person.

"Mr. Bolles," Mr. Moto said, "you must not mind it, please."

"Mind what?" Bob Bolles asked him.

"That you are so unfortunate as to have killed that man," Mr. Moto said. "When it is over, so unpleasant."

"You mean," Bob asked him, "that you mind a thing like that?"

Mr. Moto laughed in a pleasant social way.

"Sometimes yes and sometimes no. Mr. Kingman really was very, very nice. I hope you are not disturbed."

"No," Bob Bolles said, "not at the bottom of me. I guess I'm getting tough."

"Oh, no," said Mr. Moto. "You are developing, please. If this lasted longer I should be afraid of you, I think," and Mr. Moto laughed.

"I don't believe it," Bob said, "but it makes me feel better to hear you say it, a whole lot better."

And it was true. He felt better about himself than he had for a long while. The palm-leaf huts by the old pier were black and deserted in the moonlight. The people must have run into the bush again when they had heard their steps and voices; and they walked past the huts without speaking and down to the beach. The water was silvery in the moonlight and by the breakers there was a fiery phosphorescent glow.

"So very nice, the moon and water," Mr. Moto said. "Now we will build a fire, please. Here are some matches, Mr. Bolles."

There was enough small wood on the beach to build a fire. In five minutes it was burning brightly and all their faces were clear in the firelight.

"If Tom's out there," Bob said, "he won't be able to get through the reef until morning."

"I have a suggestion, please," Mr. Moto said. "I should like so much to be able to close my eyes. It will be so nice if you and Mrs. Kingman will give me your word not to leave the beach. I trust you, Mr. Bolles. Please, I treat you like one of us."

"Don't say that," said Mrs. Kingman. "He isn't one of us."

Mr. Moto sat down and placed his arms across his knees and rested his head upon them. Bob Bolles wanted to ask him if his shoulder hurt, but he did not. Instead he walked with Mrs. Kingman a little distance from the fire.

"Do you think he's all right?" Bob Bolles asked her.

"Yes," Mrs. Kingman answered. "It was in the shoulder. I helped him fix it. It hurts of course, but it's all right. Why, what are you laughing at?"

"I was just thinking," Bob said.

"What were you thinking about?"

"I was just thinking," Bob told her, "what I'm going to tell the boys on the *Smedley* if I see them."

"Don't," she whispered, and she looked at Mr. Moto sitting near the fire. "Don't talk about it now."

Then they sat down on the sand with their faces toward the sea. They just sat there not speaking for a long while.

"You're not angry with me," she asked, "because I . . . ?" She stopped. "The knife — I had to do it." And he knew what she meant.

"No," he said, "you had to. I can see a lot of things more clearly than I ever did before. I never realized before that there are some things more important than any two people or the way they feel. I've always been pretty egotistical, I guess. It's knowing you that's changed me."

"Why!" Her whole face lighted up. Her eyes were sparkling in the moonlight. "I was so afraid you wouldn't see. Why, it's been worth while if I've done that. No matter what happens, it's something to remember."

"I thought you never liked remembering," he told her.

"Not often," she answered slowly; "but there'll be a sort of a past with you. No one can stop that. I can always think how it would be if you were there and how it would have been if I were not just what I am. Yes, I'll love to think about it always."

"I'm sorry," he said, "about what I did — spoiling everything for you. It was just the same with me — I had to."

Her hand closed over his and her grasp was strong and steady.

"Of course," she said. "It's just the same. And no

matter where you are, it's something to be proud of, something to remember. If things go bad with you you must always think — promise me you will — that you did something splendid once. Why, you beat us all, my dear — some very dangerous people. I'm sorry for myself, but not as sorry as I'm proud of you. I'm all mixed up in my mind, because I'm a woman. Women ought to be at home looking after men."

"Everything you say is new," he said, "and everything you say I like."

"You like it, dear," she said, "because it's dangerous to know me. You'll take me back tomorrow."

"Yes," he answered, "if Tom comes, anywhere you say."

"It will be Kingston," she said. "No, there will be no trouble for me there. It will be arranged and you needn't ask me how. It will take a little while to get to Kingston, won't it?"

"Yes," he said, "and that cutter may pick us up."

"Oh, no," she shook her head. "They'll have other things to think about, once they see the plane. We will have a little while on the way to Kingston. It's something, after all. You won't see me again after that. You must not even know my name. You mustn't — ever."

It had come. Perhaps he had always known it would, but when he heard her say it incisively there in the moonlight he felt the injustice of it very keenly.

"Look here," he began. "Why won't I see you?" And then he found himself believing all sorts of things which seemed true at the moment. He was begging her to leave it all. He was begging her to stay with him, but she knew better, and she was hardly listening to him.

"Under the trees," she said, "when you were going to the plane, I should have waited until your back was turned, but I couldn't. Now, do you understand?"

"That has nothing to do with you and me," he told her.

"Oh, yes," she answered, "everything. You see what I was planning?" She nodded toward the fire, but her voice was very low. "He thinks we have what we all wanted. I was planning to get it later. That would have been more important than you. I can't be different from what I am, and you can't either. Don't you see? You'll be going back to your country and I'll be going back to mine."

"We can chuck it all," he told her.

"Oh, no, we can't," she said. "You'll never mean that again — not after what you did tonight. You can look anyone in the eye and you can just remember. . . . But there's still a little while. We're not back yet."

"No," he said, "not yet." He hesitated. "When this

war is over — and it will be over sometime — I'll be looking for you. I couldn't help it."

The moonlight struck her face as she turned toward him, just as though she had moved nearer to him from the dark.

"You'll wait," she asked him, "will you?"

And he told her he would wait, and she looked surprised at first, and then she smiled.

"It's queer," she said, "I never thought of that — I mean about sometime when there might not be war — when the lights might be lit again. I live in the present — all of us have to. Perhaps it's better not to look too far ahead."

"I'll be looking for you," Bob Bolles said again.

"Will you?" she asked him again. "Well, I'll be very glad and I'll be looking for you too."

CHAPTER XIX

HE WANTED to get away, to leave there, and he was deathly afraid that Tom would not come back, but Bob Bolles saw the *Thistlewood* just a few minutes after he saw the first streaks of light on the horizon. He must have made the island in the dark and have been standing outside waiting for the morning, for almost as soon as Bob saw the silhouette, just beyond the reef, she started under power and began heading for the narrow channel. He was afraid at first that Tom might get into trouble, but Tom remembered the bearings. Tom was a good sailor. By the time the anchor splashed, the beach and the water beyond it were faintly pink in the sunrise and all three of them walked down to the water's edge. Although Mr. Moto was most polite, it was clear that he was very anxious to see the last of them. His face was several shades paler and Bob could tell that Mr. Moto's shoulder pained him.

"Come aboard and have something to eat," Bob said.

"No, thank you very much, please," Mr. Moto answered. "It is so very important for you, I think, that you should go before my friends arrive. We want no more difficulties, do we?" And Mr. Moto laughed. "Please call your boatman now. Tell him to come ashore at once, please." And Bob Bolles called to Tom across the water.

"Come on, Tom," he called. And they stood watching the dinghy come toward them. They did not speak until the bottom of the little rowboat scraped against the sand and until Tom stepped into the water and pulled the bow up on the beach.

"Well," Bob said, "I guess this is good-by. It's nice to have seen you, Mr. Moto." Then he was aware of a change in Mr. Moto's manner. Mr. Moto's smile had grown more mechanical. His eyes had grown more watchful and Bob knew there was something else. He knew it was not finished yet.

"So nice to have met you," Mr. Moto said. "Some other time again, when it is pleasanter, I hope. You must step aboard at once, please. The farther you are away so much the better for you, I think."

"All right," Bob said, and he turned to help Mrs. Kingman. "You'd better sit in the stern," he said. "Tom and I can push her off." And then Mrs. Kingman gave a sharp surprised little cry. Mr. Moto had backed away from them. He had jerked his automatic pistol from his pocket.

"Here," Bob said. "What's that for?"

Mr. Moto stood with his feet carefully braced in the sand and the clean fresh light glittered on the gold of his front teeth.

"No," he said quickly, "it is all right. Just a precaution, please, in case you should be angry at what I have to say."

"Why," said Mrs. Kingman, "why — what's that? Haven't we said everything?"

Mr. Moto shook his head at her and his voice sounded less polite.

"Mrs. Kingman, please," he said, "I kept it for the last. I hope so very much you know what I mean."

"Why, no," said Mrs. Kingman. "What do you mean?"

Mr. Moto looked down at his pistol and back at her.

"Excuse me, please," he said. "I think you have been so very nice and clever, Mrs. Kingman, through it all. I should be so sorry if you should leave thinking I was so stupid, please."

"But, Mr. Moto, I don't think you're stupid," Mrs. Kingman said.

"Oh," said Mr. Moto and he laughed, "so sorry I must be so impolite as to disagree when everyone has been so nice. You and Mr. Kingman both thought I didn't know."

"Why, Mr. Moto," Mrs. Kingman said, "know what?"

The gold in Mr. Moto's teeth glistened and he laughed, but not politely.

"It was so clever about the turbo supercharger, Mrs. Kingman," he said. "I know so very well it was not the turbo. Please do not bother to come back to get the rest of what is in the plane. I only want to say my friends and I shall get it, please. The Nipponese Intelligence is not as bad as that. It is Beam 21 A Night Combat please, Mrs. Kingman."

"Oh —" Mrs. Kingman began, but Mr. Moto stopped her.

"So sorry to distress you," Mr. Moto said, and he took a short step toward them. "That is all, I think, please. Into the boat at once. You too, Mr. Bolles. *Boy san,* push it off. Good-by."

The bottom of the dinghy grated on the sand as Tom pushed off, wading beside it. Then he stepped in and picked up the oars and began to row. From the center thwart where he was sitting Bob Bolles could see Mr. Moto still standing close to the water. Mrs. Kingman sat in the stern with her back turned toward the beach. She did not speak, but her face was lighted by a faint malicious smile and Bob could see that she was very happy.

"Good-by," Mr. Moto called. "So sorry for you, but good luck."

"Tom," Bob whispered, "put your back in it! Row like hell!"

"No," Mrs. Kingman said softly, "don't hurry. It's better he shouldn't know." Then she smiled at Bob and she seemed to have forgotten all about the island. "Look at the color of the sea," she said.

THE END